MW01105744

Room
Board
and
Murder

Room
Board
and
Murder

Phyllis W. Fravel

Author Representative
Jeanne D. Fravel
P.O. Box 1466
Dahlgren, VA 22448
USA

Production: Fourth Lloyd Productions, LLC.

ISBN: 978-0-692-92373-3

Printed in the USA

For my family, with a special thanks to Marion Wall, a good friend.

Contents

Prologue

C arley was miserable. The entire trip on the night train out of Union Station in D.C. had been miserable. She had never been able to sleep sitting up, especially on the hard woven cane seat with the unforgiving back. The grossly overweight, hairy man in the seat beside her evidently had no such hang-ups as he softly whistled and snored, his head bobbing over pudgy hands folded across his ample chest. His white, seersucker jacket was draped over the seat armrest he shared with Carley. To make matters worse, his blue cotton shirt exhibited large sweat stains under his armpit, and each time he moved his elbows a pungent aroma of body odor wafted freely towards Carley.

The dim overhead light in the coach kept Carley from seeing any of the passing scenery outside the window. Only the brightest of the stars and distant streetlights winked back occasionally. Mostly, she could only see her reflection staring back at her. Over her shoulder she noticed several riders were reading newspapers, and a few had hats pulled down over their eyes and were obviously sleeping. The coach was crowded, and Carley had nowhere to move. She felt trapped. But she was comforted in the fact she would be returning to Washington on the early evening train from Pittsburgh in a couple of days.

The six-hour trip to Pittsburgh, Pennsylvania, had not warranted a Pullman berth even if she could afford to pay. It was 1932 and the "Great Depression", as they had dubbed the passing years, was in full sway.

Carley decided to pass the time picking her brain of memories of her Grandmother Mertins, who now lay in a wood casket in the baggage car, probably impatiently waiting for her final internment in the cemetery of her hometown. Carley propped her arm on the wooden seat rest under the window and nestled her chin in the palm of her hand. Her head bumped a couple of times on the cool windowpane. She let her mind wander to yesteryear.

Grandmother Florence had been only thirty-eight years old when Carley was born, and she insisted on being called "Aunt Florence". Carley never knew her father, who, according to her mother, was a sailor who had died on the high seas during a storm. They had not married. Her mother had called Carley her "love child", and Carley felt warm at the memory. In fact, Carley realized she had never felt loved by anyone else but her mother. Surely, Aunt Florence had never loved her, and Carley couldn't remember her ever giving her a hug or even a kiss on her cheek, even when she had innocently, as a child, asked her for one. It hadn't taken her long to feel rejection, so she simply stopped trying. In fact, Aunt Florence had seldom lost a chance to remind her she was illegitimate. But her mother loved her. When Carley was about ten years old her mother died of double pneumonia. Carley had felt totally alone and kept to herself except when Aunt Florence demanded she attend to a chore.

Aunt Florence, Carley remembered, had been the youngest of nine children born in a poor coal mining family in southwestern Pennsylvania. When Aunt Florence was four, her mother had died giving birth to a stillborn baby boy.

Florence had been brought up by siblings. By the time she was fourteen, she had decided to run away.

Both of her sisters married and were raising children of their own. One of her brothers had left home for the steel mills of Pittsburgh, and the others drudged home, black-faced and beaten down after hours in the coal mine.

Aunt Florence had taken the opportunity of going with a carnival when she was barely fifteen. When it stopped in Pittsburgh, she left them to become a kitchen maid in a home of a very wealthy man and his family. For two years, she learned all she could about proper manners, speech, cooking and reading. A loving, older housekeeper took her under her care to teach her to read and to aspire for something more than the life of a servant in someone else's house.

One summer, the Mertins' family, old friends of her employer, came to visit for a month. By the time a week had passed, their son, Cornelius, had found himself captivated by Florence's shy flirtation. By the end of three weeks, the two eloped to Fairmont, West Virginia, where one dollar bought a marriage license and two bought a yellow wedding ring. A sympathetic minister performed the nuptials.

The Mertins weren't too happy about the situation, but Florence did her best to be lady-like and agreeable.

Life had been a social one, with frequent teas and parties that suited Florence just fine. A daughter, Evelyn, was born a year later. But tragedy struck when Carley's Greatpa Mertins went broke. Aunt Florence had told Carley it was because of bad business, gambling and loose women. Luckily, Great

Grandmother had her own bundle of stocks and cash as life went on until Great Grandpa died of a heart attack.

Great Grandmother Mertins passed soon after, leaving Carley's grandparents, Cornelius and Florence, sole owners of the Mertins Mansion. Cornelius, however, had to work, something he had never been acquainted with. Unfortunately, he soon died in an accident when he fell down an open elevator shaft while hauling lumber in a warehouse.

Aunt Florence had to be resourceful. Her only skills were those learned at the Pittsburgh house prior to marriage; she looked around D.C. and decided to open a boarding house. Invitations to society events had immediately ceased upon Cornelius' demise. Carley guessed it was Aunt Florence's temperament, but, of course, Aunt Florence laid it to a wayward child with a bastard grandchild. Carley was already working at the florist when the 1929 stock exchange crash left as useless paper the few remaining stocks Aunt Florence had.

No wonder, Carley thought, Aunt Florence was such a bitter, unloving person. She must have felt she couldn't rely on anyone. She was alone, save one brother, Samuel, who had infrequent correspondence with her. It was through him that Carley found out there was a burial plot available in Pennsylvania.

Aunt Florence had left the world a week ago after a three-story fall down the stairwell of the spiral staircase at her boarding house. Her neck broken, she still held in her hand the unbroken light bulb that she had been attempting to put in the overhead fixture above the stairwell. Carley smiled to herself. Aunt Florence would have been glad it was unbroken, because she was a champion at squeezing a quarter until the eagle on the back peed.

No, Carley didn't have warm feelings about her grandmother, and while she was not glad she was dead, she was certain someone was. Carley was *dead* certain Aunt Florence had been murdered.

One

The piercing brass gongs on the good old reliable Big Ben alarm clock jangled Carley awake at 6:00 A.M. in the morning after she had arrived home from Pittsburgh. At first she had felt like a stranger in her own home, for she had moved her clothes and other belongings from her tiny third-floor room to Aunt Florence's bedroom on the first floor.

Most of her grandmother's belongings had been boxed up and banished to the attic. Carley's bags and boxes sat in chairs and stood at attention on the floor. A few of her garments had been hung in the large chifferobe and the deep closet, the only one in the room.

Sorting out and putting away comes later, Carley thought, right now it is time to get to work in the kitchen. Donning a blue printed cotton housedress, she hurried to the kitchen through the door at the rear of the dining room. As she put white linen napkins and silverware in front of each seat at the big, round, mahogany table with one thick, round leg in the center instead of legs, she kept an ear turned to the squeaky gate at the rear of the garden where Frances and Tillie Jones would appear around seven o'clock. Mother and daughter, they had worked for Aunt Florence for several years as housemaids and meal servers. Indeed, Tillie had only been a child of ten when she first began working after school and on weekends. They would work a twelve-hour day seven days a week for seven dollars each. It was considered good wages, especially since they ate three meals each day at the boarding house.

Carley struck a lucifer on the sandpaper side of the matchbox she had taken from the shelf above the oven. She turned on the knobs for each gas burner and then lit them. Blue flames leaped high. She put the coffee percolator on one, the teakettle on another, and then she poured cold milk for the cereal into a large ceramic pitcher with colorful tulips on the sides.

Looking up through the window, she saw the two women stepping across the red brick garden walk, their heads together in what seemed a secret. Frances, tall and busty, looked strong enough to lift a piano all by herself. Tillie was as tall as her mother, but slender and wiry.

"Good morning, ladies." Carley welcomed them.

"Mornin', Miss Carley." Tillie smiled as she put her big tan burlap bag on the floor under the stove. Frances did the same with hers. They both put on crisp white bib-aprons and got ready to serve the boarders as they came down for breakfast.

Carley thumbed through the breakfast menu orders each boarder left by their plate for the following day's breakfast. A couple preferred corn flakes or shredded wheat to eggs and toast. They had no such choice at lunch or dinner but ate, or not, what was set before them.

Carley cracked eggs for an omelet while Tillie made toast

in the new pop-up toaster as Frances counted link sausages into the big, black iron skillet. The oven had been turned to low heat to keep warm each portion of the meal that was ready. Tillie filled jelly and marmalade bowls and placed them on the table along with a plate holding a slab of tub butter and a silver butter knife.

"Oh, my," Tillie's eyes widened, "lovely flowers on the table! Ol'Missus Mertins never put flowers on the table."

"They were selling a bunch for fifteen cents at the train station when I got in last night. They kind of beckoned to me. I like flowers." Carley exclaimed.

"Missus Mertins," explained Tillie, "would never have done that. She never picked the garden flowers for the house, either."

"There's going to be a lot of changes around here. I think you'll like them. First, I'm going to sit at the table with our boarders. I want to get to know who's in my home."

Neither Aunt Florence nor Carley had ever sat down with "strangers", as Aunt Florence called them. She considered herself above people who had to pay for a place to live. At that moment, Bill Wampler, the blind border, and his seeing-eye-dog, Buddy, came through the dining room and into the kitchen on their way to the back door to let Buddy out for his morning romp and constitutional. Tillie opened the door for them. Bill, a short, tubby man dressed in his white office shirt with a blue bow tie, turned back to return to the dining room. Swinging his cane to feel his way, he caught Carley's ankles, causing her to fall to the floor, tossing a box of Post Toasties flakes into the air. Carley found herself sitting on the linoleum covered with breakfast food.

"What happened?" Bill's voice piped.

"Oh, Miss Carley," Tillie laughed and then slapped her hand over her mouth.

"Hush, child," Frances glared at her daughter. "Do you want to get us fired?" But she had a hard time trying to suppress a smile herself.

Again, Bill Wampler anxiously asked, "Did I trip you up, Miss Mertins? I'm so sorry. So very sorry."

Carley scrambled to her feet and wrapped her arms around him. "It's all right. It was more my fault than yours. I know by now to look out for your cane." She gave him a quick squeeze as Bill almost purred.

"Oh, my, Miss Mertins, I haven't been hugged like that since . . . I can't remember when. Thank you."

"Please call me Carley, Mr. Wampler, since we live in the same house we should be on a first name basis. Don't you think?"

Bill smiled. "Well, since I dumped you on the floor, I guess we're not formal anymore, are we?"

"Guess not. Now, go sit at the table and Tillie will get your breakfast for you."

Frances swept up the cereal flakes from the floor and tossed them out the door for the birds. Carley dismissed the blind man from her list of miscreants. First, she thought him too nice. Second, he lived on the first floor and had probably never been to the second floor, let alone the third floor. Somebody would have seen him coming down with his cane, or Buddy, the morning of Aunt Florence's demise. No, Carley reasoned, not Bill Wampler. Buddy scratched at the back door and Carley let him in. He promptly walked over to Bill's chair and curled up at his feet.

As Carley returned to her duties, she heard Tillie telling Bill that his juice was at twelve o'clock, his coffee was at one o'clock, and his eggs were on the right-hand side of his plate with his butter and toast on the left.

"Do you want marmalade or grape jelly," she heard Tillie ask.

"None for me," Bill said.

Carley thought to herself, "Not the blind boarder."

Two

"Miss Carley!" Tillie's shrill voice reverberated through the dining room to the kitchen where Carley was wrist deep in yeast dough.

"What is it, Tillie?"

"There's a policeman at the front door that wants to speak with you."

"Well, don't let him stand there in the vestibule. Show him in and seat him at the table and pour each of us a cup of coffee."

A red-haired officer in full uniform strolled in, his right hand extended, his hat tucked under his left arm.

"Sorry, can't shake yet." Carley said. "I'm in the middle of making bread rolls for dinner . . . won't be long. Have a seat."

"No hurry, Miss Mertins. Just wanted to welcome you as the new head of the house and let you know I have the day shift for this beat for the next couple of months."

"You're Officer Clanahan, aren't you?" Carley asked. When he nodded his head she continued. "Weren't you the officer on duty a couple of weeks ago, when Aunt Florence died? I was at work at Goodman's Florist when it happened and didn't get back here before you had already gone. Your name was mentioned."

"Yes, but obviously, we didn't get a chance to talk then. Sorry about your Aunt."

"Actually, my Grandmother, but that's all right."

Carley pinched off just enough dough to make a roll and then placed it in a larded and floured rectangular tin pan. One by one the rolls filled the tin, and the mother dough mound disappeared. Two dozen rolls sat side by side, and Carley covered them with a warm damp cloth to help the yeast in them rise. She washed her hands and wiped the butcher block table that she had been using to knead the dough. The table stood in the alcove where a working fireplace had once served as a stove and supplied heat to keep the kitchen warm. A few hooks still dangled from the bricks where black pots once held water, soups and stews.

"Tillie, while we're talking would you and your mother please clean the third-floor bedroom that used to be mine? Clean it thoroughly and put in clean linen. I want to put a vacancy sign in the window."

"Yes'm," Tillie said almost dancing out of the kitchen.

"She seems happy," Officer Clanahan observed.

"She usually is. She and her mother are good people." Carley poured them both a fresh cup of coffee before she sat down. He had finished his first cup and hers had cooled as she made the rolls. "I do want to talk to you about the events . . . the accident. What everyone calls "an accident"; I understand you were the first outsider in the house after it happened."

"Yes, Ma'am, I was. But please, call me Terry. Here's my card with my badge number on it." He laid the card down on the red checkered cloth in front of her cup. "I don't feel like a stranger to you. I've seen you come and go when I happened to be on 18th Street, when you went to work while I was on my beat."

"Well," Carley took a deep breath, her elbows on the table, holding her coffee mug in both hands. "I don't believe it was an accident. I believe Aunt Florence was murdered; pushed over the rail by someone who wanted her dead. Probably out of spite for the way they were treated."

Terry emitted a soft whistle as he leaned back in the wooden ladder-back chair and pondered what Carley had just said. Scratching through his unruly carrot curls, he thought through the facts as he knew them. He found himself looking deep into Carley's green eyes and had to shake his head to bring himself back to the matter at hand.

"Now, why would you think that?"

"For one thing, Aunt Florence had changed the bulb in that fixture at least once a year. I've seen her carefully, very carefully, step on the short ladder one rung at a time and put her hand very carefully—the one without the bulb—on the low ceiling to secure herself. She never made a quick move in her life. She hadn't reached out, since the old bulb was still in the fixture and the new one was still in her hand. I'm certain she was pushed over the rail."

"I see," Terry took a pencil from his shirt pocket along with a small pad of paper from the inside pocket of his uniform jacket. "I can understand your reasoning. I'll give it some serious thought."

"That's all I can ask," Carley smiled. "For now."

A sharp knock at the kitchen door got their attention. Eulali West stood there with money in her hand. Eulali had been a flapper in the "Roaring Twenties", as the decade had been dubbed, and had reluctantly updated her wardrobe to the more sedate thirties. Her chubby legs were clad in black lace hose and the black line was impeccably straight. Her toes were wrapped in black patent pumps with jeweled ankle straps.

"Miss Carley," Eulali said, her eyes on Terry. "Here's my next month's board money. I need a receipt. Hello, Terry," she smiled, her eyes darting between the two young people.

Carley rose and went to a drawer under the dish closet where she kept a cigar box she used for cash and receipts. She filled out a receipt and handed it to Eulali in exchange for four ten-dollar bills. "You know Officer Clanahan?" she asked.

"Oh, yes, we're old friends," Eulali said as she turned on her high heels and exited through the dining room into the hall. They heard the front door close behind her.

"Miss West seems a nice person," Carley said returning to her seat. "But a bit flamboyant with that "Betty Boop" hairdo and all the jewelry she wears; but she must be really nice to take care of that old man at night until his daughter gets . . . ."

Carley didn't get a chance to finish her remark for Terry had choked on a gulp of his coffee. Carley jumped up and slapped his back until he got his breath back. She realized he was laughing so hard that tears were in his eyes. "Now, what did I say that was so funny?" she demanded, hands on her hips.

"Eulali—Eulali doesn't care for an old man at night, she's a. . ." Terry tried to find the right words.

"She's a what?" Carley gasped and put her hands to her mouth. "You don't mean she's a . . ." Carley couldn't put her thoughts into words.

"No, no," Terry slapped his knee. "She's not a street walker."

"That's a relief," Carley sighed as she walked over to the rolls and shoved them into the oven. "Then what does she do?" She asked impatiently.

"She works at the Gayety Theater," Terry smiled.

"The Gay . . . that burlesque theater down on Seventh Street? She's a strip-tease dancer?" Carley couldn't believe where the conversation had gone.

"No, she's a wardrobe mother there."

"What's that?" she asked.

"She sews up tears, takes tucks and keeps the costumes clean. Adds sparkles to the pasties."

"Pasties?"

Terry blushed and said, "You really don't need to know. The girls all love her and give her all that jewelry. It's not real. Just stage stuff, but it's real pretty."

"If Aunt Florence had known, she would have put Eulali out in the snow in winter," she laughed. "By the way, how do you know all this?"

Terry sniffed the air. "Those rolls are sure smelling good."

"They'll be done soon, but you'll have to wait until they cool a bit before you can eat one. Too hot out of the oven gives you a tummy ache. Now, you didn't answer my question."

"This beat around here hasn't been my only one. We are alternated every few months. Downtown can be pretty rough at night. Now, in Chinatown there's violence you'll never hear about for they take care of their own problems. Florida Avenue gives us a busy night, but it's usually drunks out in the street. There are lots of bars and clubs along that strip. One good place is Howard Theater. Lots of class there.

"Where do you like best?" Carley folded a couple of towels and used them as pot holders to lift the hot pan of rolls from the oven. She took a lump of butter and used it to shine the tops of the golden-brown rolls. "Have you driven a police car or worked in Precinct 6?" She grabbed a small blue and white plate from the shelf and with a small spatula put two rolls on it.

"Yes to both," Terry's eyes zoned in on the plate set before him. "But I like hitting the bricks, as we call the beat. Get to know the folks you serve."

Terry couldn't wait and took a bite of one of his rolls. It burned his tongue. He took a gulp of his cooled coffee before eating the rest, and putting the second roll in his clean handkerchief. He excused himself. "I have to report in on the call box on the corner. I'll see you soon."

When Terry had left through the back gate, Carley considered Eulali. It was a big "if", but maybe Aunt Florence had found out about the Gayety, and what Eulali did for a living. She probably had threatened her or ordered her to leave. Well, it could be a motive!

Three

"Well, look at you," Carley stood back and viewed Peter Robert's spiffy new uniform. Tall and darkly handsome, he looked like a movie star in his tan bus driver's outfit. He had on a pair of jodhpurs, leather leggings and a Buster Brown belt that put a strap up over his shoulder through an epaulet. Under his left arm he held a tan visor cap.

"I've a new route," he explained proudly. "I'll have lots of tourists riding. My new bus is a double decker with a speaking tube to the upper deck. Gotta tell my riders all about the landmarks we go past. I go past the Lincoln Memorial, the Washington Monument and the Pan American Building to name a few historic sites."

"What do you tell them that they don't already know? They know what they're seeing, don't they?"

"Oh, I have a book to memorize that has a lot of interesting facts about just every building you might go past in D. C."

"I'll have to take a ride on your bus someday. Give me a copy of your schedule when you think about it, please."

"Did you know there is a house on 16th Street that has

seven kitchens?" Peter asked barely keeping a straight face.

"Seven kitchens?" Carley asked innocently, "Why so many?"

"Gotcha," Peter grinned, "Mr. and Mrs. Kitchen live there with their four kids." Then he became serious. "Miss Mertins," he asked softly, "I don't have but thirty dollars for next month's board. Can you wait? Or maybe I can fix something for you? I'm a pretty good handyman, or so I've been told. I fixed a few things for your grandmother, but she only gave me fifty cents or a dollar."

"Well, I do have need for a man around the house, as it were," Carley said slowly, seriously considering the offer.

Peter smiled broadly; obviously relieved that he might have a chance to keep more of the two-thirds of his fifteen dollar a week salary that he would otherwise spend for room and board.

"That railing on the third floor hasn't been put to right. I could do that."

"All right. You do that—but in the daytime while no one's sleeping. And not when your bus schedule is during the day."

"And Miss Mertins, would you mind if I looked around the house for cubby holes and such? Old houses are very interesting to me, especially those that knew the Civil War. They sometimes have places where slaves heading North through the Underground Railroad were hidden. These houses have stories to tell if you can find them."

Carley smiled at his almost childlike enthusiasm. "I don't mind as long as you don't disturb anyone. Rented rooms are not to be entered. Go ahead and poke around any other place though."

"I understand, Miss Mertins."

"How do you intend finding these 'hidey holes'?"

"I just tap around with a little metal hammer I have."

"Well, tap away … but quietly."

"If I find anything, I'll let you know before I tear into it." Peter was quick to assure Carley. "And thank you, Miss Mertins."

"Please call me Carley. Miss Mertins makes me feel old. Like my grandmother."

"Okay, but only if I am Peter to you."

Before Carley could agree, a shriek from the kitchen sent them both running. Sitting in the old oak rocking chair by the sink was Frances with a baby blue jay cuddled in the warm brown cleavage of her ample bust. Tillie had opened the screen door on her way out to put trash in the large galvanized can on the back stoop, and the little blue nestling, just barely flying, mistook the bosom for his nest. He promptly made himself at home and opened his mouth wide for a worm from his momma. Unfortunately, Frances was not the one the little nestling needed.

"Oh my, little one," Frances smiled. "You need your own nest."

"If I may," Peter blushed, "I'll take the wee one back to

where it belongs." He tenderly picked the nestling up and placed it in his warm broad hands and went out the door to the big oak beside the rose garden along the side fence.

A couple of minutes passed and then . . . "What in the world," Carley exclaimed as a cacophony of angry cussing made her put her hands over her ears to shut out language that was fairly turning the air blue.

Frances put her hands over her ears and ordered Tillie to do the same. Tillie complied, her eyes wide, trying hard not to laugh. Peter was flailing his hands around his head and sprinting for the back door. "Dammit, you SOB, I ought to tear out your nest and kill you all!"

"Peter, what on earth is the matter?" Carley met him at the door and saw blood streaming down the side of his face intermingled with sweat from the June heat.

"I think I know what happened," Frances said, reaching for Peter and sitting him in the rocking chair she had just vacated. "There's no fury like a daddy or mommy blue jay when it thinks its baby is in danger. My, he pecked you real good, didn't he?"

"Tillie, get me some turpentine and iodine out of the medicine cabinet in the bath." Carley ordered.

Tillie jumped away from the ironing board where she was smoothing pillow cases and hurried to the bath.

Carley dipped a clean white cloth in some warm sudsy lye soap water and carefully bathed the wound. Peter flinched and held his breath.

"He got you real good, but the iodine will heal and the turpentine will make a good scab."

Peter shuttered and squealed "ouch" as the iodine met his proud flesh. "There's no blood on my uniform, is there?" he asked anxiously.

Carley took a good look and pronounced his attire untainted and Peter sighed a visible sigh of relief.

"Thank you for rescuing that baby bird, but I didn't know you knew all those words, let alone you would use them!"

"Sorry, Miss…er, Carley. I can't believe I used them within earshot of ladies, either." His eyes swept around the room including both Frances and Tillie.

"I guess you had pretty good cause," Carley said. "We'll forget it. There, the bleeding has stopped. Be very careful when combing your hair for a couple of weeks. Your cap will cover the wound so no one else will notice. Do you have time to sit down to lunch? We're having potato soup and sliced bologna and tomato sandwiches."

"Sounds good, but I'm almost late as it is," Peter said. "I'll be back for dinner though." He put his cap on very carefully and gave a quick salute as he left.

Carley felt a bit anxious as she mulled over the morning's events. Peter had seemed so helpful and pleasant, but he certainly had a bad temper. She wondered if he and Aunt Florence had more than words on the third floor. Carley decided she would tell Terry about Peter's temperament.

Four

Carley fingered through the small ring of keys Aunt Florence used to carry hanging on a long string looped around her neck and tucked into her apron pocket. As she searched, Frances and Tillie stood quietly by waiting for the day's orders.

"Ah, here 'tis." Carley triumphantly held up a long, slim skeleton key. "This goes to the French doors to the ballroom off the main hall. That room has been closed up for decades. Aunt Florence didn't want boarders to use the room, and she didn't want the expense of cleaning it."

"I'se knows I've never been in there." Tillie smiled, obviously curious as to what was behind the fancy glass doors with curtains on the other side.

"I'm going to open it up to the boarders so they can have someplace other than their rooms to sit and read in the evenings or in the afternoons, for that matter. And they can play chess or checkers or cards and enjoy what little time they have away from their work."

"Gee, but that's nice." Frances gushed with a broad smile on her face, "Missus Mertins never thought about other people's feelin's like you do."

Carley felt a little guilty, for her main reason for opening the room was to eavesdrop on conversations that might lead her to finding out who had pushed Aunt Florence over the railing.

"See that it's spic and span. I'll take some of the house-keeping chores upstairs for a week or two to give you time to clean it thoroughly."

They stepped from the kitchen and walked through the dining room passing the huge, dark mahogany highboy with its mirror reflecting sparkling crystal cruets and candle hold-ers proudly lined up to reflect. The sun sent sparkling, danc-ing colors across the ceiling. Over the highboy hung three framed paintings . . . one, a large oval, and two rectangular. The smaller two depicted bowls of peaches, apples, grapes and limes against a drapery background, and the middle oval showed a poor dead goose hanging by its legs midst a few branches of wheat and oats.

"As a child," Carley stopped to look at them and smiled, "I always hung my head when passing through here. I al-ways felt so sorry for that poor goose hanging by its dead feet, even though it was hung with all those pretty grains and berries."

Frances laughed. "That would seem pretty gruesome for a little girl."

Walking briskly, they soon came to the hall and faced the glassed double doors that were covered with sheer ecru curtains inside the room. Carley put the key into the hole, turned it, and pushed the doors open. A musty smell greet-ed them as they stepped through into the large room whose twelve-foot ceiling was furnished with one large chandelier. Rococo plaster moldings seemed to hold up the ceiling and push back the walls.

The floor was covered with oriental rugs that showed a bit of wear in some spots. Two huge white marble fireplaces, resplendent with grapevines and grapes, pressed themselves against the further wall holding up gilt-framed mirrors that reached to the ceiling. The fire cavity itself had been closed shut with gleaming white tile. This had been done when the furnace had been installed, and the fireplaces were no longer needed. Carley stopped short for a moment remembering way back when the warmth of a fire had blushed her face when she sat cross-legged on the hearth eating a roasted marshmallow.

"I loved this room as a little child. I played under the tables and sat in the window seats and watched the world go by. The streetcar stop was on the corner over there," she pointed to the window. "And I watched the same people get on and off each day and made up stories about them. They never knew I was there. At least I don't think they did." Carley grinned mischievously.

"Window seats?" Tillie exclaimed looking around the room. "Where?"

Carley walked over to the front of the room where three shuttered windows took up the wall from floor to ceiling. She opened the shutters to reveal sills several inches deep facing tall windows looking out upon 18th Street and the cobblestoned road with streetcar tracks cutting a silvery rail down the center.

A couple of wispy spider webs hung from the upper corner, and Frances quickly took a dust rag from her apron pocket to wipe them away.

"Law's, Miss Carley, there's two pianos in this room!" Tillie gasped. "An' two big sofas an' tables an' chairs, too!"

"This room used to be host to musicals and all kinds of socials. Yes, until the bad times. No one came over after that. But that's a tale best left untold today. Now, I know you've noticed all the beautiful china vases and porcelain figurines. They are so dear and precious to me, so take especial good care of them as you wash them. Look up, Tillie, and you'll see your first order of business."

Tillie and Frances both stared up at the chandelier hanging in the middle of the ceiling. Crystal droplets hung in layers from a large circle to a point making up the fifth layer.

"How do we clean that?" Tillie asked anxiously.

"It's not really hard. First, you move all the furniture from under it, and then, spread newspapers thick on the floor. Get the tall stepladder and take up a bucket of warm ammonia suds with a soft brush and then dip each crystal until it's clean. Then you pour out the dirty water and get a bucket of clear clean water and go up and rinse each one. Then you let it drip dry on the newspapers. Of course in the meantime, she who isn't dipping crystals is dusting and waxing furniture. The last thing is using the Hoover to vacuum the rugs. See how simple it is?" Carley shrugged her shoulders as if the duty would be a snap.

"Yes'm, Miss Carley," Frances said, rolling eyes skyward. "Sounds like a lot of fun." She grinned at Tillie. "Especially that part about not having to change the beds for a spell."

"Just make it a short spell, and we'll all be happy." Carley walked back to the French doors and handed Frances the key. "You're the keeper of the guard . . . make certain it's locked up when you come out to help serve meals."

As they stepped into the hallway, Carley's eyes were drawn to the spot below the banister where Aunt Florence's body had lain after her fall down the stairwell. A table stood there with fresh flowers cut from the garden every couple of days. Her thoughts were cut short by the clamor of feet racing down the circular stair from the third floor. Upon seeing the ladies looking up, Wilbur Foucher, one of the boarders, stopped at the top of the last set of steps and then slowly descended to the hall floor.

"Good morning, Miss Carley . . . ladies." Wilbur greeted them. "Looks like it'll be a gorgeous day."

He was a little gnome of a man with black unruly hair making him five foot eight inches in height. His neatly trimmed black mustache framed his nostrils as it pointed upward to his almost yellow eyes. He always wore a black suit with white shirt and black ribbon tie.

"What do you have there?" Carley asked as he lifted a leather bag filled with four rolled up canvases that fell out slapping the wood floor.

"Oops!" Wilbur stopped to pick up the pictures he had painted in oil. Carley knew he was setting out to sell them on the streets or in offices all over town—as far as his legs would take him.

"Let's see what you have before you take off for the afternoon." She reached down and picked up a still life of a vase on velvet drape with some roses laid beside it as if someone were ready to arrange them.

"They're really quite good, Wilbur. What do you think you'll get for this one?"

"I'm hoping maybe fifteen or twenty each except for the big landscape; I'd want at least fifty for that one. I might get that in an office someplace."

"Well, good luck. See you at dinner?" Carley asked rolling up the last of them and tucking them back into the bag. Wilbur nodded in affirmation. The ladies watched as he pushed through the heavy stippled light oak door into the vestibule. Carley smiled to herself.

As Wilbur's form disappeared down the front steps, Carley came to the conclusion he couldn't have killed her Grandmother. He was too sweet, too soft spoken and an artist with an artist's soul, she was sure. Yet, she had recognized the vase in his painting as one from the den on the second floor. It had been gone for a while and then someone, obviously Wilbur, had put it back where it belonged. Had Aunt Florence found out and . . . no . . . Wilbur would have gotten the worse part of any confrontation, Carley was certain. No . . . not Wilbur.

"Those windows are awfully dirty . . . 'spec'ly on the outside." Frances observed.

"I don't want you ladies washing windows outside. Would your man, Jolie, do them?" Carley asked Frances. "I'd pay him by the window. He can do them as extra money along with the yard work."

Jolie Jones had been keeping the yard and surrounding

shrubbery in tiptop shape for years. Aunt Florence had depended on him to do small repair jobs, too. Sometimes she just paid him with an extra meal or so.

Frances quickly offered Jolie's services. "Sure, he would agree to the bargain readily . . . or else!"

"Poor Jolie doesn't even own his own soul, does he?" Carley laughed.

"He's a good man and God has blessed me with him and Jolie knows I feel that way. We're good for each other." Frances smiled a bit sheepishly.

A jangle of the front bell sent Tillie to answer. When she opened the door she found Terry standing there with two large brown grocery bags; one in his left arm and one at his feet.

"Here, take this." He handed one to Tillie and reached down for the other for Frances, who had come up behind her daughter.

"I just got back from Edinburg, Virginia, and my folks' place that is on Creek Road. They have a small farm there . . . a couple of pigs and cows . . . and a large vegetable garden. I told them how kind you've been in feeding me every so often . . . well, more often than not, and they wanted me to bring these to you. Corn, tomatoes, beans and I think a couple of summer squash . . . the yellow kind.

"How nice." Carley peeked into the top of one of the bags. "Here, take them to the kitchen, and we'll think of how to use them tonight. Sliced tomatoes would sure taste good. Of course, you'll stay." It wasn't a question; it was a decided statement Carley made for him.

"How was your visit and how did you get there?" Carley inquired knowing Terry didn't have a vehicle to drive.

"I went by Greyhound and walked up Creek Road," Terry began to explain. "It's only a couple of miles, and then I took the bus back. People looked a little funny at me for the vegetable bags, but lots of them had bags of some sort with them."

There was an awkward silence between them as they stood for a moment looking into each other's eyes. A warm smile turned into a broad grin on Terry's face. "Hey, there. The Fourth of July is coming up soon, and I was wondering if we could go to the Washington Monument to see the fireworks together."

"Is that a statement or an invitation?" Carley teased. "If it's an invitation, I accept. I'll bring a basket dinner, and we can eat first and get us a good seat. Fireworks don't start until nine."

Terry beamed. "And do you know what?

"No, what?"

"We can plan on a picnic sometimes in Rock Creek Park and . . . ."

"Whoa . . . " Carley laughed. "I can't get away . . . you know that."

"Of course you can. We can arrange it somehow, can't we ladies?" He grinned at Frances and Tillie and they rolled their eyes up to the ceiling with smiles showing white teeth in their dark faces.

"We'll see," Carley started lifting tomatoes from the bag

exclaiming how lovely they were. "Are you sure they've given excess and not what they need? This is a lot!"

"Mom has already canned over seventy-five quarts of tomatoes along with that many green beans, carrots and I can't say what else. She's already giving to the church's vegetable stand in nearby Woodstock, where the needy come and just get whatever they need.

Most all the farmers around there do the same. Sure helps those who haven't gardens or jobs in these days."

"We'll be sure to thank her . . . or better, give me her phone number and I'll call."

"Oh, she doesn't have a phone. In an emergency I can call the firehouse, and they'll get a message to her."

"Then I'll write her. Give me her address."

"I told Mom I was going sparking with you and she was tickled pink. She wants to meet you and says to bring you down home soon."

"Whoa there. Not so fast. You must understand that nothing can come of this. We can't get serious about anything . . . just have a little fun and companionship, that's all."

Terry looked a bit shocked at Carley's declaration but held his tongues. "Okay, but we'll talk more about this later."

"Yes," she said, ". . . later."

Five

"'The Lord's in His Heavenly Mansion and all's right on His earth' . . . or however that quote goes . . . and Miss Carley, just look at you! Your smile would light up the darkest gloom." Horace Owens smiled broadly as he gently pushed Beatrice's chair under the table. "You look lovely this morning."

"Watch it there," Peter grinned. "Your wife is within earshot of you flirting with another lady."

"Oh, I don't mind, Peter. It's just his way. We've been married a little over forty years and he's never once said a cross word to me."

"You never gave me a reason to, Dearie." Horace said with a smile.

"He is a charmer, Beatrice." Carley smiled at the grey-haired lady. Although in her sixties, her complexion was both smooth, without wrinkles, and still what was termed "peaches and cream".

"He has to be in his business. Selling insurance takes a lot of diplomacy and good will. Nobody would buy if the salesman didn't have a smile on his face."

"So you sell insurance," Peter said, stuffing a hunk of

sausage into his mouth. "Never knew what you did when you left the house after breakfast."

"He goes house to house mostly collecting the premiums each week. He has a pretty big clientele," Beatrice explained proudly.

"Surely you don't do all that walking with him, do you?" Carley looked alarmed.

"Oh, no. I visit my twin sister, Bonnie, who lives on New York Avenue. She is very ill . . . has been for years. Her husband, George, is a salesman at Woodie's Department Store. That's where Horace gets all his suits, like this tan striped seersucker he's wearing. Gets them on sale and with an employee discount."

Horace stood up straight and took a whirl fingering the maroon bow tie at his neck. The way his wavy white hair topped his tanned skin made him seem younger than his years.

Carley chuckled and turned her attention to Beatrice, "What do you do all day with Bonnie?"

"Mostly we sit around and chat all day, but on Wednesdays we have a couple of friends in to play bridge and have tea. Bonnie's daughter, Janet, is a nurse at Sibley Hospital. She doesn't get home usually until five o'clock in the evening. George doesn't get home until almost seven o'clock. I usually fix eats for Bonnie and sometimes start dinner for Janet and George. Horace wanders in and out during the day whenever he can."

Silence fell over the room as they attended to eating their breakfast, and only the occasional clinking of silverware interrupted their thoughts. Suddenly, Carley tapped her cup with her spoon. "I almost forgot to tell you. I am going to make up picnic baskets for the Fourth of July. It's only a couple of days away, and I thought you would like to go down to the Mall to see the fireworks and floats and to hear the bands in the parade. You don't have to take your basket, if you don't want to. You can eat it here, but if you do take it please bring them back, so I can use them again."

"You don't have to make one for me." Eulali said. "We'll have a celebration down at the theater. We can see the fireworks from the stage door."

"Before I forget." Carley smiled, pushing back from the table, "The big room in front has been opened up for you all to use. Tillie and Frances have been cleaning all week to make certain every dust bunny and spider web have disappeared. That room used to be a ballroom where my ancestors held musicals and people danced, sang and really had a wonderful time. I hope you will be able to enjoy the room and that you will try to keep your hot ashes off the carpet. Maybe one day we can have some parties in there. I only ask you to try to be very quiet after nine or ten o'clock so no one's sleep will be disturbed."

"Can we invite guests over?" Eulali asked, jiggling her bracelets in emphasis of each word.

"Of course, but no liquor is to be served in that room. There's a player piano in there and the big drawer under the settee in the hallway is filled with music rolls for it. I tried one out the other day, and it worked fine. In the window seat, there are games like Checkers, Chess and Parcheesi.

Help yourself to any of them, but put them back when you are finished with them."

Thoughtful silence permeated the dining room, and Carley sensed the air fill with deep thought.

⌒

With the dishes cleared away and water sloshing into the iron sink in the kitchen, Frances approached Carley who was seated at the table thumbing through recipes.

"Can I talk to you for a minute, Miss Carley?"

"Of course, what's up?"

"Well, I just want you to know Tillie is getting married in a couple of weeks.   She's the first one in my family to get married in a church. Jolie and me, well, we jumped the broom down in Atlanta almost twenty-five years ago. Never did stand up to a preacher. I took his name, and we had four chillums, three boys and Tillie. She's eighteen now . . . finished high school, and I'm right proud of her. Will you come to the wedding?"

"Of course I will. Wouldn't miss it for the world."

"I was hopin' you'd say that. Old Missus Mertins . . . well, I wouldn't even ask her. She thought we's dirty. Never touched us. Put our pay on the table for us to pick up . . . no ma'am she never touched us . . . no ma'am."

Carley watched Frances' back, as she bent to push her hands into the hot water and suds. Maybe, she thought, Frances did have reason to push grandma over the railing after all!

Before Carley had a chance to say anything more to Frances, Wilbur came into the kitchen carrying a screen cage.

He held it up to show the ladies what he had. "I made this so I can put a cocoon in it. There's a butterfly cocoon hanging in the tree down the street. When the time is right, it'll be a beautiful butterfly."

"And what are you going to do with it?" Carley asked curiously.

"I'm going to paint a pretty picture. Then I'll let it go. I shouldn't have it in the cage more than a few hours."

"I'll be anxious to see the picture. Be sure to show me when it's finished."

"I will, Miss Carley." Wilbur turned, almost skipping out of the room.

Carley and Frances shared a chuckle as they watched him go from the room dangling the little screen cage. Wilbur seems such a child in spite of a little grey creeping into his black lead of hair. "Yes, he seemed so innocent," Carley mused.

Six

C arley was walking toward her bedroom intent on cleaning out all the drawers and nooks and crannies she
hadn't had time to put in order to her liking in the month
since Aunt Florence's death . . . or murder, she reminded
herself. Most of Aunt Florence's clothes had already been
boxed up and sent to the attic, but shelves and small drawers had barely been investigated. Before she could turn the
knob in her hand the doorbell rang, and knowing both Frances and Tillie were at the grocery store, she walked swiftly
across the entrance hall and opened the front door. Standing in the vestibule were two people; a very tall young man
clad in knickers, argyle knee socks and holding a soft visor
cap in his large knuckled hands, and a small woman with
grey hair partially covered with a wide brimmed straw hat.
She wore a cotton yellow print dress with buttons down the
front and grasped a large cloth purse. Before Carley could
greet them, the lady announced she was Mrs. Weldon Keller
and the young man beside her was her son, Buford.

"We stayed at the Y.M.C.A., across the street, last night
and saw your sign in the window. Buford has won a full
scholarship to George Washington University," she proudly
announced to the obvious discomfiture of her offspring.

"We want a room within walking distance. I don't want him in a dormitory setting ... too much distraction from studies."

When Carley got a word in pretty much edgewise, she asked them to enter the hall and took them up to the third floor to the room she had occupied until recently.

"It looks nice and clean with ample space for his belongings," Mrs. Keller announced after a swift but thorough exploration of doors and drawers. "How much do you charge?"

"Ten dollars a week . . . or forty a month. That includes clean sheets, pillow cases and washcloths and towels each week and three meals a day, if he is here. I could fix him a bag lunch of a sandwich and fruit or cookies, if you want."

"That's fine. Oh yes, this is a Christian home, is it not?" Mrs. Keller's eyebrows rose inquiringly.

Carley dropped her gaze to her hands and then looked up trying not to smile too broadly at Buford's mother's concerns. "Well, frankly, I don't know if all my tenants are Christian or not. I've never asked them for I don't really consider it my business. As long as they don't commit any crimes or outwardly cause quarrels concerning religion . . . and, of course, pay their rents, I don't ask."

"Well, I guess that's alright. He'll be looking for a church in the next couple of weeks before classes start. There are some nearby, aren't there?" she asked, and then added, "Or would you know?"

"Oh yes," Carley let the almost snide remark pass her by. "There is a Methodist church on H Street and the New York

Presbyterian Church just four blocks down. I understand President Abraham Lincoln went there."

Mrs. Keller put her freckled hand deep into her purse and brought out a small leather change purse in which several bills were wadded up. She pulled off several and counted out a hundred and twenty dollars. "This is for the first three months and, if he stays, I'll send you payments every three months for as long as he stays. Is that satisfactory?"

Carley accepted the bills and turned to go down the stairs. "I'll write you a receipt and give it to you before you leave. I'll be in the kitchen . . . just knock on the jamb if you can't see me. It's right through the dining room." Carley left Mrs. Keller sorting through the items in her son's luggage and placing them in what she thought was their proper place.

Carley gave up any hopes of sorting through her own room until her new boarder and his mother had gotten him settled, and she was on her way. She felt as though she hadn't gotten much information from the mother but looked forward to talking to the son . . . if, indeed he talked! So far, he hadn't uttered a sound except to grunt when he hauled his heavy bags up the stairs to his room.

It wasn't long before a knock was heard at the kitchen door, and Mrs. Keller said she had to catch the Greyhound bus back to Morgantown, Pennsylvania, and that she would be in touch with her son often and perhaps visit at Christmas. All this had been said in a rush, and she turned on her heels and marched . . . yes, that was the word Carley decided . . . marched out the front door.

Carley checked on a few things in the ballroom to make certain Frances and Tillie had emptied the smoke stands of pipe plugs and ashes, the newspapers were smoothed and folded on the glove table behind the maroon and tan striped divan. She glanced up the stairs where she could see the door to the Keller room. It was shut when she had gone into the ballroom, and it was still shut when she came out.

As she walked down the entrance hall toward the dining room, she heard the door open and quick steps tapped down the wood floor to the carpeted steps. Looking up, she could hardly believe her eyes. A young man in long pants, short-sleeved polo shirt and canvas shoes smiled down at her.

"Hello, there," his warm baritone voice greeted her. "I'm pretty much settled in. I think I'll just take a walk around the neighborhood before lunch. I want to go past the White House and see a few of the historical facades. It's a beautiful day."

"Well, Buford . . . I hope I can use your first name, you'll . . . ."

"Actually I hope you'll use my nickname 'Bucky' instead of my first name. Mother hates my nickname which the kids at school gave me, but I like it and prefer it." With that he all but skipped out the door and was soon gone from view.

Well, Carley thought to herself. Bucky it is, and what Mama doesn't know won't hurt her. I bet he doesn't wear knickers and argyle socks anymore, either.

Frances and Tillie came in the back door loaded with groceries from the A & P grocery store on G Street in the

McReynolds apartment building. "Why didn't you get the delivery boy to bring all that in his wagon?" Carley asked.

"It would have cost you a nickel tip, and besides, we're able to carry 'em."

"Well, thank you ladies for thinking about my pocket-book, but I do know that poor boy's mother could probably use the five cents more than we need it."

"Mebbe so." Tillie grunted, placing a heavy bag of canned veggies on the red checkered tablecloth. "But your Grandmother would send us back for two or three trips if we couldn't carry everything—before she would think of paying a delivery boy. She never gives any delivery man a tip for their service, even at Christmas when they kind of depend on people to be generous so their families can have a little extra."

"Well, we won't think about what Aunt Florence did . . . we'll just do what we think is best from now on.

While you were gone, we got a new boarder. His name is Buford . . . Bucky Keller. He'll be going to the University in a few weeks. His mother came with him to get him settled and paid for three months. I suppose you'll meet him at dinner. He's out getting acquainted with the neighborhood."

"What are we having for dinner?" Tillie asked.

"Salad and drivel soup. I have the potatoes and onions already cooked, and I put in some diced ham. I'll make the drivel noodles just before we serve. There's both cake and pie left over from the weekend festivities, and they can have their choice pretty much. In the meantime, I'm going to try to do some organizing in my room, if you need me."

Carley closed the door quietly and leaned her back against it, surveying the room she had occupied for only a few weeks. The walls were plastered white, dingy from years of being neglected, and she envisioned them with wallpaper in the design of latticed pink roses and green leaves from top to bottom. The ugly brown burlap textured drapes would have to go, to be replaced by filmy white curtains and a tan velveteen valance. Perhaps the dark wood doors would be painted cream. Her eyes fell to the ratty looking bedspread. She took one quick stride to the side of the bed and flung it into a pile on the floor. My, how liberating it was to really do away with the past . . . the stifling past . . . and make this room her own.

Sitting on the side of the bed, now covered only with clean white sheets, she reached into the bottom drawer of the night table, on which a single brass-stem lamp held a bulb that did little to lighten the room, because the lampshade looked like it had been soaked in linseed oil. It probably had, for Aunt Florence believed the oil kept mosquitoes away. The drawer surprisingly held a metal grey box with a small padlock. Carley found a small key taped under it.

When she opened the lid she whooped at seeing a pile of money and some jewelry and a small ledger. She counted the money and found more than two thousand dollars. The ledger totaled the amount, as money earned by the business of boarders and the sale of a couple of jewelry items. Carley was dumbfounded. She had no idea Aunt Florence had any savings at all. "She always talked so poor-in-the-mouth," Carley mumbled to herself.

Carley picked up the jewelry . . . a necklace and a brace-let of pearls and rubies. As she fingered them, she noticed a piece of paper stuck in the corner of the metal box. Tears came to her eyes as she read the words written in her moth-er's hand. "Carley, my dear daughter. These are not real gems, but they are pretty and will dress up anything you wear. I want you to have them on your eighteenth birthday. Love, Mother."

Had Aunt Florence forgotten to give them to her? No, of course not . . . she saw them every time she opened the box to put in more money and write in her ledger. A wave of renewed resentment against her dead grandmother swept over Carley, as she put the pearls around her neck and slipped the ruby and gold bracelet on her arm. She stretched out across the bed and looked up to the ceiling.

Well, Aunt Florence. Thank you for the money. It will re-decorate this room, and remove even the smell of you from it. One day, maybe, I'll even forget you entirely. I hope.

After searching every closet, drawer and nook and cranny in the room, Carley put several items, including the drapes, into cardboard boxes and piled them in the hall.

"Frances . . . Tillie come here."

When the two ladies came out of the dining room into the hall and stood in front of her, Carley pointed to the box-es. "I want you to take these things, and also all of Mrs. Mertins things we packed up in the attic, and give them to anyone you know who can use them. In these days of need it would be a shame to hold on to what I can't and probably never will need."

"Oh, Miss Carley, thank you so . . . so much. I know just the folks who can use most anything."

"Don't thank me . . . thank Aunt Florence . . . maybe if she can hear her things are being put to good use, it will do her some good, too."

"I wouldn't count on that too much, Miss Carley, I just wouldn't," Frances smiled.

"Nor would I," Carley said to herself as she turned to go back into her room and plan on the next steps she would take to make "Mertins Mansion" her own.

Seven

Carley stepped into the kitchen and looked at the bank calendar hanging on the wall, aware that today marked her first month anniversary of taking over the mansion since Aunt Florence's death.

July Fourth dawned in brilliant sunshine and found Jolie sitting at the kitchen table slurping on the rim of a cup of very hot coffee. He had just helped Carley hang two American flags from poles jutting out from a couple of the second floor windows. A bunting of red, white and blue draped over the front door in celebration of the country's one hundred fifty-sixth years of independence.

"Did you notice the beautiful swags hanging from the top floor of the Powhatan Hotel?" Frances asked, referring to the tall building at one corner of 18th and Pennsylvania Avenue.

"Sure did, honey." Jolie grinned as Tillie laid a plate of steaming yellow omelet and hash-browned potatoes down before him. "The whole town's all decorated up in red, white and blue and stars everywhere."

Carley laid her empty plate on the sink board in the corner of the room. "Frances, I think there are a couple of dishes in the dining room to bring out, and see if Bill wants more coffee."

She then turned her attention to Jolie. "Thanks, again, Jolie, for helping me this morning. You were a great help. Do I owe you anything?"

"No'm. Glad to do it and this good brek'fus is plenty thanks. Is there anythin' else I can do 'fore I head out?"

"No, I don't think so. Are you planning on watching the parade downtown this afternoon?"

"Oh, yes'm. We have several nieces and nephews we're gonna take along. Nothin' like seeing a parade through a child's eyes."

"Never thought of it that way, Jolie, but you are right. Well, have a good time. I'll hear about it from Frances and Tillie tomorrow, I'm certain."

When the house had quieted down and a lunch buffet had been set out, Carley turned her thoughts to outfitting the picnic baskets for the evening. As she placed a name tag on each one, her thoughts went back to wondering which one of them pushed Aunt Florence over the third-floor railing. Of course, not Bill Wampler . . . he had never been above the first floor and, besides, he was much too sweet tempered . . . she ruled out Beatrice who was too caring a person and also too frail.

Of the rest . . . well, Peter did have a terrible temper and Eulali was no shrinking violet. Horace was a sweet talker, but he was too good to be true, she thought. That left Wilbur, the little elf-like artist with a soft spot for poor but-terflies, and Frances and Tillie, who had never said a hateful thing about their former employer, even though Carley was certain there had been many times when they would have been almost justified.

She put the napkins in the baskets along with paper plates, kitchen knives, forks and spoons and little salt shakers. Then she set about cutting up chickens to fry, peeling cooked white potatoes and chopping onions for salad. She had made coleslaw the previous day and homemade white bread rolls would round out the meal. For dessert, she decided to include a piece of the angel food or sponge cake in each basket. "They can purchase a bottle of pop from a vendor on the avenue," she mused.

"Something sure smells good." Terry stepped into the kitchen from the backyard. "Don't suppose I could get an early bite of that cake, could I?"

"No . . . you'll have to wait with the rest of us or there might not be enough cake to go around. We had it for dessert last night, too."

"All the more reason why I should sample it ... everyone else has!" Terry reasoned.

"Oh, well, go ahead, but only a little bitty piece. By the way, have you come to any conclusion about who might have done the dastardly deed on Aunt Florence?"

"Assuming there was such a deed?" Terry smiled. "You're determined aren't you? I've talked to everyone at some time or another and, short of asking the question, 'Did you do it?' I really don't know."

Carley decided not to argue the point; at least not at the moment. She took the boiling spuds off the burner and ran cold water over them to stop the cooking. She had cooked a dozen eggs earlier, and she started peeling and chopping them, along with the onions to blend with mayonnaise for the salad. She planned on putting little half-pint canning jars filled with salad and slaw in each basket with a tangerine to round out the meal.

"What time did you want to start down to the festivities?" Carley asked.

"I'd like to see the street entertainment about five o'clock," Terry said. "Is that okay with you?"

She nodded in agreement.

⌒

The afternoon was long in the tooth before the last basket had been picked up from the dining room table by the boarders anxious to get down to the Mall where they could see the fireworks.

Frances and Tillie had gone home as soon as they had put out the buffet lunch consisting of sandwich makings at 11:00 A.M.

"I bought that Ford roadster my friend, Paul, wanted to sell." Terry told Carley as they left the boarding house. "Its several years old, but I think I made a good deal. Besides, I love to work on cars. Maybe one day I'll open a garage, if I ever get tired of being an officer of the law."

They strolled down past the White House on Pennsylvania Avenue, jostling pedestrians hurrying in the same direction. Across the street in Lafayette Park all the benches were occupied by people feeding squirrels with peanuts purchased from the vendor on the corner. His little steam whistle on his cart beckoned one and all to come buy his peanuts and roasted chestnuts.

A few more city blocks down 15th Street brought them to Constitution Avenue where earlier the big parade with magnificent floats and marching school bands from Virginia, Maryland and the District had thrilled the crowds lining the sidewalks. Vendors hawked their wares from carts as Terry and Carley found a place in the grass near the Washington Monument to spread their lunch cloth and sit down to eat their meal while many families did the same.

"Still smells good." Terry grinned gripping a chicken leg in his hand. "Can I look forward to cooking like this after we're married?"

"Whoa! When did I ever say we were to get married?" Carley protested.

"Well, you didn't, but you will. You just cannot resist my charm. Seriously, will you marry me?" Terry took Carley's hand and quickly slipped a ring with a small diamond on it.

Carley shook her head sadly and took the ring off and handed in back to him.

"You don't understand, Terry. I won't . . . can't, marry anyone. It's not you, believe me. I just can't . . . shouldn't marry anybody."

"No . . . I don't understand. Explain so I can." Terry spoke in almost whispered tones rolling the ring over and over in his palm, looking deep into her eyes.

Carley took a deep breath and then said in a low voice barely audible above the mumbling of the crowd around them. "Because I'm a b-b-bastard."

"A what?" Terry asked.

"An illegitimate child. You know. My mother and father were never married. Aunt Florence said I should never marry because no child should be brought into the world knowing her mother was . . . a bastard!"

"Stop right there," Terry smiled. "If anything, it was your parents who were acting so-called illegitimately, not you. You had nothing to do with it. I certainly don't care, and I doubt that once we're married and have kids, the first question anyone is going to ask is if your folks had stood up before a minister in a church and taken vows of marriage."

Carley was silent for a long time, as Terry kept holding her hand and slipped the ring back on her finger.

"It's a lot more, Terry. I fear I come from a family of total losers. Oh yes, my great grandfather built the mansion that is now the boarding house. It used to be the scene for society balls and parties and grandiose living. However, . . . it seems he liked to play cards and bet on horses and spend lots of money on loose women," Carley sighed, her eyes dropping to her left hand, "Or, so Aunt Florence used to tell me. What a heritage that would be for our children." Carley fell silent in deep thought, twisting the ring around her finger trying to decide if she would take it off again.

Terry clamped his fingers over her hand and with the long finger of his other hand, lifted her chin so he could look deep into her eyes. "Carley, darling, I'll not take 'No' for an answer. Somewhere in my past, sure and begorrah, I'm certain we have one or two, maybe more, bastards. And we've had more than our share of drunkards, failures and ladies men. So, you see all your protests don't mean a thing to me. You are going to marry me . . . and that's that. Now let's finish this wonderful meal you prepared for your husband to be."

Carley looked up into his eyes and had to remind herself she was in public, or she would have thrown herself on him in shameless abandon.

As she looked up into the air and saw the first sparkles and heard the crackle of the fireworks display, she could not help but think of independence . . . independence from her Aunt Florence's vitriolic condemnation of her mother and herself, innocent as she was of any moral wrongdoing. Carley felt free of that burden, and tears of happiness filled her eyes.

Eight

Frightened shrieks filled the whole house at two o'clock in the morning, as Carley jumped from her bed, jamming her feet into her satin slippers and pulling on the pink chenille robe which hung from the bedpost. The sound of stamping feet added to the noise of the night. By the time Carley had reached the bottom of the stairs, someone had already started pounding on the door adding to the cacophony.

"Eulali! Wake up! You're having a nightmare again! You read one of those horror stories again last night, didn't you?" Peter stood in front of the door and continued to knock loudly.

The screeching stopped, and they heard Eulali jump down from her bed and paddle over to the door. While she slowly opened the door and peaked out, everyone relaxed. The Owenses had only opened their door from the adjacent room, peeped out, and then retreated back into the room.

Carley muttered, "Oh, no," upon seeing Bucky cautiously creep down the stairs from the third floor. What a greeting on the first week at the boarding house. I hope he doesn't decide to leave, she thought.

The door opened and Eulali stood there in a red flannel robe, her face plastered with cold cream and a heavy white net tied tight over her black hair. She certainly didn't look like the Eulali of the light of day.

Eulali loved horror stories and murder mysteries. She would buy the dime novels every chance she got. She had stacks of them in her room. Every so often, she would have to get rid of them when the rental license inspector would come. He calls them a "fire hazard".

Carley looked up the steps to see Wilbur Foucher sitting on the top step with Bucky. His gestures assured her that he was explaining the situation, for Bucky broke out in a broad smile, and slapped his knee and started to rise from the step on his way back to his room. Wilbur, then, braced himself against the railing and hoisted himself to his feet, and went back up to his own room, his shoulders shaking from the retained laughter.

When Carley turned to go back down the stairs, Bill and Buddy were standing in the hallway looking up.

"Show's over, Bill," Carley laughed. "It was Eulali having a nightmare again. I do wish she'd stop reading those books so late at night."

Bill giggled and patted Buddy on the head then shuffled back to his room, yawning widely with his hand over his mouth.

Carley smiled at Peter as he did a quick salute before disappearing back into his room. Eulali, then, shut her own door quickly.

With a deep sigh, Carley entered her own room, hung her

robe on the bedpost and kicked off her slippers. She snuggled under the covers and promptly went back to sleep.

⌐

At breakfast, Eulali looked a bit sheepish as everyone gathered around the table. Of course, except for Bucky, everyone had gone through the early morning events before and really thought nothing about it.

"Good morning, Miss Eulali," Bucky said.

"Good morning, Bucky. I hope you were able to get back to sleep."

"Yes, I did. And if you don't mind, I'd like to borrow some of those books you read. Mother never approved of me reading anything other than the classics, but once in a while a friend of mine from school would put one on my desk for me. I'd keep it in my locker and read it at lunch time. I love them."

"You're welcome to have as many as you want. I never reread them and can only sell them back to the bookstore for a penny when I've collected too many."

"Where do you work?" he asked innocently.

"I work down at the burlesque theater as a stage mother." Eulali answered truthfully.

"A what kind of theater? I don't think we have that in Morgantown."

"You'd love it. Lots of happy music and girls that dance on stage with men that tell all kinds of jokes to make you laugh so hard you'll cry. Would you like to come sometime?"

"You bet I would! It sounds like lots of fun. How much does it cost? Bucky asked with a slight hesitation in his voice.

"I tell you what," Eulali smiled. "I'll give you a back door pass. Come around to the alley door and show it to the man there. Tell him that I sent you, and you'll get right in."

"Gosh, that's good of you. When's the best time?" Bucky asked, with a note of urgency in his voice.

"Friday nights are best. Guys seem to take their girls out to restaurants or movie houses on Friday nights, so the Gayety isn't so crowded. I'll get the pass for you tomorrow. Remind me."

This isn't the road Mother Keller would have Bucky go down, Carley thought. But after looking at the boy, she decided not only was it not her job to look after him, but also the experience might be good for him. She could only pray he would keep his eyes on the road that would lead to a doctor's stethoscope.

⌐

Terry came charging through the back door and grabbed a cup from the cupboard and poured himself some coffee. He turned to Carley and took her left hand and held it to his lips. As he bent to give it a kiss, he stopped as a surprised look covered his face. He jerked his head erect and stared at Carley.

"Where's the ring?" he demanded.

Carley held onto his hand and pulled him back through the screen door into the garden. "It's right here." Carley pulled a gold chain from her bosom with the sparkling ring dangling.

"I never said I would marry you, if you remember. I'm not saying I won't, but I'm not quite ready to announce it to the world. Do you mind? I'll either give it back to you, or one day you'll see it back on my finger."

Terry stood still, his head hung in thought then looked up in a smile. "Of course, it's okay. I don't want to rush you. I want you to be good and sure you want to be Mrs. Clanahan. I wouldn't want you to regret it later. Although, I am ready to meet the preacher today."

"Thank you, Terry. Let's get back inside. I have breakfast to get on the table. Can you join us?"

"No. Gotta get out on the street. Wouldn't want to get reported malingering on the job. See you later today." Carley reached up and gave him a kiss on the cheek. Terry fairly skipped down the garden path and through the back gate. Carley turned back into the house to find both Frances and Tillie working hard but giving each other sly looks with knowing grins.

"All right, girls," Carley said. "Who wants cereal this morning?"

Nine

The murmur of voices from around the breakfast table floated into the kitchen where Carley was putting on a second pot of coffee. Terry had stopped by earlier and had had two full cups before heading out to his beat. Horace Owens knocked on the door jamb and cleared his throat, getting Carley's attention.

"Horace . . . what can I do for you?" Carley asked, turning from the stove.

"Well," Horace hesitated almost wringing his hands, "Beatrice is not feeling at all well this morning, and I was wondering if I can take her breakfast up to her."

"Of course you can." She turned to face toward Frances who was busy getting butter from the refrigerator. "Frances, do you know if we have a bed tray? I think I remember one somewhere."

"Yes'm. I think there's one upstairs in the maid's room. Last time it was used was years ago when Old Missus had that carbuncle and had to stay in bed with a doctor. Remember?"

Carley almost laughed at the thought of Aunt Florence in bed with the doctor but checked herself upon seeing Horace's distraught face.

"Oh, yes, very well. Go get it, and if it's in good shape, we'll use it."

Frances went up the bare board back steps leading behind the back wall of the kitchen to a hall on the second floor and another flight of steps to the third floor. The stairs led directly into a dingy room with two small windows and a bare bulb hanging from the ceiling. Frances pulled the light switch chain and the dull illumination was hardly better than no lighting at all. The view from the windows overlooked the backyard and the alley. Looking over the room, Frances saw the tray on top of the dusty wood table with one wood chair beside it. A single bed with a mattress on top of bare springs and a clothes closet were the only other pieces of furniture in the rug-less gloomy room. Before starting back down the steps with the tray, Frances noticed cobwebs on the upper windows and determined to come back up and get rid of them. She hated spiders. She shuddered and then descended the back steps to the kitchen with the tray.

Horace was telling Carley that Beatrice had been feeling poor for a few days.

"I called Bonnie and got George on the phone. He said he would get a neighbor to look in on Bonnie for a few days. Neither of the ladies like complaining. I really think Beatrice has been feeling worse than she told me this morning. It's just her way."

"Scrub that tray thoroughly, Frances. No use taking up more germs. I'll make Beatrice some hot oatmeal and send up some brown sugar and cream. She always takes tea instead of coffee, doesn't she?"

"Yes. And maybe a couple of those biscuits with grape jelly."

"Do you want to take your breakfast upstairs, too?"

"No, I'll be back down for mine soon as I get Lovey settled."

"We'll keep yours hot for you," Carley smiled putting a clean linen napkin beside the bowl on the tray. "Is this enough?"

"I think it's more than enough," Horace smiled. "And thank you." He hurried through the dining room and hall and climbed the stairs to his room.

⌒

Carley stirred the lean ground beef with a long wooden spoon over a high flame until it had browned. She poured two quarts of homemade tomato puree over it, added several cups of chopped green peppers and onions, and a quart of tomato juice. Turning the flame to low, she put the lid on the pot, gave it a pat with her fingers and turned away from the stove. The spaghetti sauce lent an aroma of Old Italy to the room.

"Ladies," she announced to Frances and Tillie, "We're going to add a few chores to the roster for a while. And don't look so surprised."

Both ladies had stopped doing the lunch dishes to look her way. "First, we haven't cleared out all the kitchen shelves. They need new liners and more convenient arrangement for spices and boxes and cans. Even some of the things we use every day aren't handy."

"Now, Peter is doing my bedroom over . . . painting door frames and window frames and wallpapering. I think I'll have him redo the maid's room. I can rent it out in the summer to the tourists who only want to stay for a day or two without board. That project can wait until cooler weather. For now, let's concentrate on the kitchen."

"That sounds like a good plan," Frances agreed. "I sure wouldn't want to do much work up in that little room until it cools down a bit."

Tillie shrugged her shoulders. "I'll go up and kill the spiders if you want me to," she offered.

"No need. They've been happy up there for years not bothering anyone. Let's leave them alone for now." Carley picked up her purse and started toward the door. "I'm going over to the A & P and see if they have any pretty shelf liner. If they don't, I'll go on downtown to Murphy's. The shelves have been lined with cut-up brown paper bags or even newspaper. If I remember correctly, Aunt Florence wouldn't pay the few cents it would take for rolls of shelf paper."

"No Ma'am, she wouldn't . . . but then a few years back being real close with a dime was a good thing." Frances said in Aunt Florence's defense.

"Well, things aren't quite so tight now, and we need to brighten up this kitchen. In fact, I think I'll have Peter re-do the trim." Carley tucked her purse under her left arm then turned and counted the number of shelves needing decoration before heading out the door.

"Be sure to give the sauce a stir every once in a while to keep it from sticking." Carley called back over her shoulder.

On the herringboned brick sidewalk of 18th Street she hurried to the corner. As she turned, intent on her mission, she was startled when someone grabbed her elbow.

"Hold up! Where you hurrying to?" Terry asked.

"Oh! I didn't see you. My aim is the A & P—to get some shelf paper for the kitchen. You on the job?"

"Yes, I still have a couple of hours. Can I have dinner with you this evening?"

"Of course, if you like spaghetti with meat sauce." Carley felt Terry's arm go across her shoulder as they walked across the street and down the block to the store. Somehow she felt the possession Terry felt by this simple gesture of affection. Instead of feeling threatened, she realized she felt warm and protected.

"I want to tell the world that you're the gal I intend to marry."

"You're pretty sure of yourself, aren't you?"

"Uh huh, but more importantly, I'm very sure of my love for you . . . and if you love me even half as much, we'll be fine."

Carley smiled and pushed his arm away and ducked into the open glass door of the store, turned and waved at him as she turned to the long wood counter where Adam, the store manager, stood waiting for her order. The aroma of fresh ground Red Circle coffee assailed her nose from the grinder standing at the further end of the store. Glass jars full of cookies and saltine crackers stood on a shelf in the center of the store along with a big barrel standing on the floor filled with large dill pickles.

"What can I do for you, Miss Mertins?" Adam stood beside the cash register, both hands splayed in front of him making Carley think of the spiders in the upper bedroom.

"Do you have rolls of shelf paper?"

"I have several kinds." He moved quickly from behind the counter and soon returned with four rolls. One was plain white, another was striped, and a third was covered with little blue flowers that had a scalloped edge that would hang over the edge of the shelf. Carley never looked at the fourth, for she fell in love with the blue flowers and asked for the number of rolls she needed. She hadn't even asked the cost. It was the most expensive, she found out, but Carley didn't care . . . it was worth it! She knew she'd have her spirits lifted every time she walked into the kitchen.

She took a longing look at the cookies with the icing in the glass jar but decided she had all the ingredients at home she needed to make her own.

She stepped into the hot late July heat disappointed not to see Terry waiting there for her. She looked up and down the street, but Terry was nowhere to be seen. Feeling a warm breeze, she looked skyward and saw a dark cloud threatening the sunlight, and a low rumble of thunder put some hurry into her step to get under cover before the summer storm broke upon her. As she stepped through the door at the mansion, a spate of raindrops slapped against the side of the house.

By the time Carley stepped into the kitchen, the storm was unleashing torrents of rain urgently needed by the dry garden, and she could see the trees and bushes whipping

side to side in a dance of thanks for the thirst quenching
drink of water.

"Made it just in time," Tillie laughed, "just a couple more
minutes and you'd been drowned."

Frances agreed, reaching for Carley's package. "Let's see
what you have here."

Carley looked around the kitchen and saw the contents
of several shelves sitting on the table, the butcher block and
the steps going up to the second floor. Only half the shelves
were empty. The waste basket near the door was filled with
brown paper. The aroma of the spaghetti sauce drew her to
the stove where she took the wood spoon and dipped it in
and took a sip to test whether it needed more salt or pepper.
Deeming it just right, she returned the lid and turned back
to the ladies "oohing" and "ahhing" over her selection of
shelf paper.

"Miss Carley! It's lovely." Tillie exclaimed. "I can hardly
wait to see it put on the shelves."

"Let's finish empting them. We can stack things on the
floor and throw out what we know is too old. We'll probably be surprised at how much room we might have left."

They worked almost silently until Frances gasped, "Miss
Carley . . . look at this!" She climbed down the short ladder
and handed Carley a small brown bottle covered with sticky
dust, "An' it's got a skull and cross-bones on the label."

"Let's see," Carley reached for the bottle. "It's arsenic!"

"That's terrible poison, isn't it?" Tillie said in a low
shocked voice.

"Where did it come from?" Carley looked up toward the shelves.

"Way up," Frances pointed toward the highest shelf. "Tucked in the very back. I almost didn't see it. I kind of felt it up there." Her eyes rolled upward to indicate the location.

"Why would anyone . . . why would Old Missus have a bottle of poison?" Tillie looked puzzled.

"I'm sure it's quite innocent," Carley smiled. "You see, old folks used to use arsenic as a cure for boils and carbuncles. They used a very tiny bit for a few days, and it would kill whatever bad germ was causing them. In a few days they would get well. I remember when I was a little girl Aunt Florence had a terrible carbuncle on her hip. Perhaps the doctor prescribed it for her. I don't know."

"Who took care of the boarders while she was so ill?" Frances asked.

"She didn't have boarders then. My mother had just died a few months before, and Aunt Florence didn't have boarding roomers yet. That was about twenty years ago."

"You mean that poison has been up there all this time?" Tillie shuddered in disbelief.

"Guess so, but we're not putting it back up there." Carley said as she pulled the cork from the neck of the bottle and stepped out into the slacking rain to the storm drain at the end of the brick walk in the garden. She poured the liquid down the sewer, and watched the storm runoff swirl to the Potomac River miles away from the garden. "It will be so diluted that it will be harmless to anything living in the river," she explained. She tossed the empty bottle in the metal trash can to be set on the curb for collection the next day.

"Goodbye and good riddance," Carley laughed. What a day this has been so far, she thought. She hurried back into the kitchen to help wash the shelves and keep the spaghetti dinner on schedule. She dismissed the arsenic as an unnecessary topic to take up time thinking about. She had other weighty thoughts, like who could have caused Aunt Florence to fall over the third-floor railing.

Ten

"Miss Carley! Miss Carley!" Tillie's excitement swept down the stairs through the dining room and into the kitchen, where Carley sat in the red straight back chair next to the table trying to reconcile her checkbook with the bank statement.

"What is it?" Carley looked up as Tillie swept in the room.

"They're bugs all over Mr. Foucher's room. Thousands and thousands and thousands an . . . ."

"What kind?" Carley was walking at a quick pace just short of running. "What kind of bugs?" she repeated.

"I don't really know, but they're hopping and flying all over."

On reaching the third floor she carefully opened the door and peeked in. Tillie was right. There were thousands of bugs and Carley broke out in a relieved laughter.

"It's all right," she put her arm around Tillie's shaking shoulders. "They're praying mantis. It seems Mr. Foucher's butterfly cocoon wasn't a butterfly after all. The babies are so small they can go right through that screen he made the cage out of. They went right through it."

All the time she was talking, Carley was opening both windows in the corner of the room and setting the oscillating fan to blow toward them.

"What are you doing?" Tillie looked skeptical.

"The windows are open and within a short while the room will be bug free. They will swarm toward sunlight, and soon, they'll be out in the garden where they belong."

"I've never seen them out there."

"They stay pretty much hidden in the bushes where they eat other bugs as they grow up."

"There's so many of them," Tillie murmured. Carley could see her disbelief.

"Oh, they make a good meal for the birds and other insects. Not too many of them will survive to grow up really big. Now, let's go back downstairs."

"Oh my, Miss Carley, you know everything." Tillie admired.

"Only by experience. When I was a little girl I watched a cocoon in that big boxwood out by the front steps hoping to see a butterfly and, alas, when it opened up there were all these little mantis' flying all over. I should have asked to see his cocoon when Wilbur took it up to his room. I could have told him what it was."

⌐

"Peter, after your shift tonight I would like you to go with me to estimate the paint and wallpaper I will need to buy to fix up my room." Carley told Peter as he swallowed a mouthful of corned beef and cabbage before answering.

"Sure thing, Miss Carley."

Thinking the other boarders around the table should have an explanation, Carley said, "Peter is spending part of his vacation helping me redo my grandmother's room into mine. I'd rather hire him than get a stranger. He's told me he is quite capable, and I'm satisfied that he is. When he's finished, that room will be all mine."

"How come you're so capable? Terry asked him suspiciously.

"Well, my father is a master house painter in Potomac, Maryland. And he has his journeyman's papers in wallpapering, too."

"That doesn't mean you can do it, too." Terry laughed.

"Well, no," Peter grinned well naturedly, waving off Terry's apparent concern. "But ever since I was ten years old I've spent summer vacations helping Dad on the job."

"How come you didn't become a painter?" Horace asked.

"I didn't say I liked it, did I?"

"I know what you mean," Terry smiled. "My Dad is a blacksmith and huckster farmer. Doesn't really bring in a steady payday."

"Dad recently got a contract with an office building company to redo offices as they become vacant. He ends up working a lot of weekends and nights with days idle."

"I'm just lucky you're here and can work any hour you have available," Carley said picking up her plate and silverware and heading for the kitchen. Frances, Tillie and Jolie had finished their dinners in the kitchen. The girls quickly rose and stepped into the dining room to clear the table when the diners finished their meals and left the room.

Peter and Terry stood in the corner next to the black marble fireplace in front of what Carley called her utility closet. They were out of the girl's way as they chatted while waiting for Carley.

Both men followed Carley into the bedroom and their eyes swept the four corners of the room while standing by the doorway.

"I'll move the bed, night table and chairs into the center of the room and take all my things out of the closet and put them in the middle of the bed. They'll all get covered with a drop cloth, won't they?" Carley asked.

"Yes, and Dad said we could borrow all the drop cloths and ladders and brushes we need. He'll even lend us his truck for a few days. That'll come in handy in getting what we need from the paint store and wallpaper shop."

"What a savings that will be! How will you get them? He lives miles away."

"He'll meet me at the streetcar barn at the end of the line. I'll go back home in the truck with him and fill it with the necessary things and head back here in a couple of days."

"Won't your Dad need it?" Terry's eyebrows shot up in query.

"Not for a couple of weeks. He's between jobs now, and the office building is completely rented out. If someone leaves, he'll have to go repaint, but until then he intends to take it easy and let Mom earn some money sewing."

"How did they manage to raise a family of seven?" Carley was genuinely interested.

"Mom is a seamstress and has a large clientele. She's very good, and her work is beautiful." Peter was obviously very proud of her.

"Well," Carley swept her arms around to include all the walls of the room. "What do I need?"

"You want the ceiling and cornice painted chalk white?"

"Yes, and I want the rest of the woodwork . . . the window frames, baseboard and closet trim painted a light cream or tan."

"What do you want me to do with the wood inside the closet?"

"Oh, paint it tan or cream, too."

"If I might suggest, Miss Carley, that is good cedar wood in there. I know it looks dark and murky, but a light sanding will bring back the pretty reddish tan and keep the moths out. I think all the closets in this house are probably cedar." He almost lovingly patted the wood with his hand.

"You don't fool me, Peter. You really like to work with wood, don't you?" Terry teased.

"Yes, I admit I like wood. I'd rather be a carpenter than a painter. You know, make furniture and such."

"Maybe the time will come when you can take up cabinet making as a hobby." Terry suggested.

Peter raised his eyebrows. "Maybe. Maybe one day." He took out a pencil and pad of paper and began walking off the footage of the room, mumbling to himself as he wrote down the quarts and pints of paint and rolls of wallpaper he would need.

"Where will you sleep?" Terry asked Carley.

"I'll sleep on the Chesterfield in the ballroom. I've slept there before. When I was a youngster, Aunt Florence would rent out my bedroom to a tourist who only wanted a place to stay for a night or so. Then, I'd sleep on the big overstuffed Chesterfield. It's really quite comfortable."

"Your room will smell of paint for a few days," Peter informed her.

"I have three large GE oscilating fans I'll put in there, and I'll keep the windows open as well. That should dispel paint odor in short order. I'll burn a couple sticks of incense, too."

"A few days of that should do it," Terry tried to pull one of the windows open. It was paint-stuck.

"You'll need a sharp chisel to free these up, Peter."

"I anticipated that. Pop has a couple of sharp-edged plaster spreaders that will do the trick."

"Guess you've thought of just about everything." Carley smiled.

The trio walked back into the hallway to find Wilbur Foucher standing there wringing his hands, his eyes dark with worry. "Miss Carley, I just went up to my room after dinner. I had come direct to dinner when I got home from today's selling." He almost rambled in his speech.

"Oh, yes. I know what you found in your room, and its all right."

"It is?" Wilbur's head went up and he looked her square in the face. "It is?" he repeated.

"Yes, it was just an error in judging what kind of cocoon you had found. It could very well have been the most beautiful butterfly we would ever see. Instead," she giggled, "a few thousand cute little praying mantises."

"What in the world?" Peter asked Terry who was standing there with his hands on his hips.

"Yes, what's up?" he asked.

Carley explained and then turned to Wilbur. "Are they all gone?"

"Only a few left, and I'll have them all gone before I go to bed. Thank you for understanding, Miss Carley." Wilbur turned and almost raced up the stairs to his third-floor room.

Carley chuckled softly to herself before being ushered by Peter and Terry back into the kitchen where Jolie sat drinking a grape Nehi while Frances and Tillie put the last of the clean pots and pans away.

"Jolie, Peter is refurbishing my bedroom. I don't know if he'll need any help, but will you be available if he does?" Carley asked while pouring herself a tall glass of iced tea. "Anybody want some?"

Both men shook their heads "no" and she placed the pitcher in the refrigerator.

"Yes'm, Miss Carley." Jolie said. "Frances will be glad to get rid of me while all these wedding plans are being made. I'm no good at them, an' she says I'm just in the way of their doins'."

"I'll let you know soon as I know," Peter said. "Right now, I'm going to get some sleep. I run my last owl shift tomorrow before taking time off. Night all." He waved his hand and headed for the stairs.

Carley had just snapped the light switch to "off" in the kitchen and headed through the dining room when she heard the strains of piano music coming from the ballroom. She could tell it wasn't anything from the player piano. This music was classical. "Chopin" Carley thought . . . , or maybe "Liszt". It certainly wasn't Gershwin blues or jazz. Carefully pushing open the French doors she peered in. She could hardly believe her eyes. There, seated at the grand piano, his fingers deftly caressing the ivory keys, was Bill Wampler, her blind boarder. He was playing Beethoven's "Moonlight Sonata".

Carley accidently touched a chair next to the wall, and it scraped the wood floor. Bill stopped, and his fingers lay still on the keys.

"Don't stop." Carley spoke softly, "I'll just sit here and listen. It's so lovely, and you're really quite good. I love it."

Bill placed his hands on the keys and continued on until the last beautiful chord and flourish.

"How? When did you learn to play like that?" Carley asked, amazed.

"Long story."

"Let's hear it."

"Well," he began to relay. "When I was a little boy my

folks lived next door to a family that ran a music studio. Both my folks had to work, and the lady, Mrs. Carper, would take care of me. Of course, it wasn't long before I was in the studio, and Mr. Carper was putting my hands on the keys and teaching me the scales and notes. Somehow, I loved it. I could do what a lot of people who could see could not. Mr. Carper kept telling me I was the best of his pupils . . . even the ones who could see."

"Why didn't you make a career of playing? You could do concerts, couldn't you?"

"Before that became a consideration, Mr. Carper moved away and there was no money for further piano lessons from someone else. I learned typing, instead."

"Do you play anything other than classic?"

Oh, yes. I can play pretty much anything I hear. I play gospel music at church gatherings and music heard on the radio when I visit some of my friends, and they have a piano."

Bill began playing one of Al Jolson's jazz pieces, and Carley felt like getting up to start dancing. She started to sing "California, Here I Come", but broke into laughter when she hit a sour note. They both broke out laughing.

"A pianist you are . . . a singer I'm not!" Carley said and gave Bill a hug around his shoulders.

"Miss Carley, I could really get addicted to those hugs of yours," Bill teased. He turned to the piano keys and played "Good Night Ladies", and then stood up and closed the wood cover for the keys. Buddy came to Bill's side.

Carley watched as Bill and Buddy walked slowly out the

room and down the hall to disappear behind the door to Bill's room.

"Well, well," Carley muttered to herself as she softly closed the glass French door and gave one last long look at Bill's door. She quickly stepped into her own room and shut the door, still humming "Good Night Ladies".

No, she thought, Bill Wampler was not on her list of suspects. He was too gentle and refined, wasn't he?

Eleven

If Carley and Terry had ordered a nicer summer's day, they couldn't have improved on what they had for their excursion to the Shenandoah Valley. Carley had, at first, reluctantly agreed to spend a day with Terry's folks down in the valley. But, Terry's mother had called on the phone to personally invite her. Terry had shown up early for breakfast, and both Frances and Tillie had assured Carley the day would go smoothly without her.

They were wheeling down Route 55 through Haymarket on their way to Front Royal where beautiful horses were kept and trained for Government ceremonies such as parades and funerals.

"We don't have time to sightsee today, but one day we must drive over the mountain to Luray. The views from beside the road overlooking the valley are spectacular."

"I bet they are," Carley agreed. "I've never been down this way before. The only valley I ever saw was in Pennsylvania when we drove out to the graveyard where Aunt Florence is buried. They're so heavily wooded, treetops are all you see."

They were silent for a bit and then Carley added, "Oh,

and, I've been on the streetcar to Cabin John, and we go over a deep chasm there to get to the park."

"Hey, that's where we can go for a date sometime," Terry sounded excited. "I like the rides . . . especially the roller coaster."

"My favorite, too."

"Ah, no shrinking violet. I like that. A gal with a lot of gumption and spunk."

She giggled and punched him in the arm but didn't say anything.

Passing pastures dotted with contentedly grazing cows, Carley saw a couple of deer on the edge of a stand of trees. While earlier fields had seemed dry and brown, the valley had evidently not suffered a drought. The grass was green and even sparkled in places with dew. Carley realized some of the trees were apple trees, and the deer stood on their hind legs to reach some fruit still hanging from a limb. She hugged herself in enjoyment of God's amazing nature.

"There's a gas station a couple of miles down the pike. I'll stop there to top off the tank and get us a couple of cold Cokes."

"Sounds good. I am a bit thirsty." Carley agreed.

When they stopped, Carley got out and stretched her legs. Beside the station stood a long table laden down with summer squash, corn and several kinds of apple.

"Can I get a bag of applies for your mother?" Carley asked.

"You can if you are able," Terry laughed.

"What?" Carley asked, surprised.

"I'm sorry," a contrite Terry said, "but my Mom always said that when I said 'can I' instead of 'may I'. You see the correct grammar is 'may I', but I shouldn't have corrected you. It was rude and presumptuous. Forgive me?"

"I stand corrected," Carley gave a short bow from her waist. "May I get a bag of these Grimes Golden? They're the best for pies."

The lady behind the table accepted Carley's fifty cents and put the apples in a brown paper bag. Drinking the last drop of liquid from her Coke bottle, Carley handed it back to the lady who gave Terry his two cents refund.

They were soon in Strasburg, just thirty miles from their destination, and Carley put a hand on Terry's arm.

"Stop! Right there! Look. It's Tillie's wedding gift."

"It's what?" Terry slowed the car and pulled over to a roadside stand where colorful quilts hung on a long clothesline with several tall poles keeping them from dragging on the ground. Tables were piled high with hand-crafts, including baskets and pottery. Jars of honey and chunks of honeycomb were on one table. The honeycomb was tightly wrapped in waxed paper but still a few bees buzzed around protesting the theft of their hard work.

Behind a table piled with blankets and potholders sat two women in rocking chairs, their hands still folded over their laps. They seemed content to let Carley and Terry browse over their wares without expending the energy to rise and see to their wants.

"Good morning, ladies," Carley smiled. "I'm interested

in looking at your quilt in the Wedding Ring pattern." She walked over to the quilt and examined the handiwork, turning the bottom corner over to see if the stitches followed through the layers of cloth.

"This is one of mine," the lady said proudly. She was on the chubby side and wore a bib apron that covered both her bosom and lap. A wide brim straw hat seemed to float above a head of braids woven back and forth to almost make a pillow for the back of her neck.

"Very good work," Carley examined the stitches. "That's a lot of intricate needlework. My grandmother tried to get me to learn embroidery when I was a little girl, but it was hopeless."

"You have to fall in love with sewing to be any good at it, especially quilting, for it can be tedious if you're not in the mood for it. Now, me, well . . . you wouldn't want to eat anything I'd bake. Never did take to cooking."

"How much is this quilt? I want it for a wedding gift for a young lady getting married next week."

"How appropriate," the lady smiled. "It's the Wedding Ring pattern."

"Yes, I know. That's what made us stop the car and come look at it. How much?"

"The lady clasped her hands and bowed her head as in deep thought. "I'll let you have it for forty dollars. It's a double bed size."

Carley was a bit startled at the price. She hadn't thought to go that high for a gift, but looking at the beauty of the bedcover, she knew she couldn't haggle over the price.

A breeze wafted across the road making the quilt wave to her and she smiled, certain she had made the right choice.

"Sold!" Carley smiled and reached into her purse and pulled out four ten dollar bills which she handed to the lady who was reaching for white tissue paper. The lady stood on tiptoe to take the clothespins off the line, and the quilt dropped across her arms. Wrapping the quilt in tissue and then newspaper, she wrapped it with twine and handed to Carley who lovingly hugged the package. Terry reached for it and placed it in the back seat of the car.

"I got Mom some honey. They used to have a hive of their own, but a certain curious little kid got stung pretty bad one day, and they sold the hive to some people about five miles away. The doctor said he could have died."

"That's scary. But aren't you afraid to come into my garden? There are plenty of flowers and lots of bees."

"Worth the risk to see you." Terry grinned. "Besides, most bees are very passive unless you threaten them. If you leave them alone, they'll do the same."

"Well, I hope so."

"I bet Tillie will be tickled to get that quilt," Terry opened the car door for Carley to get in and then walked around to the driver's side and slid in behind the wheel. "When is Tillie's big day?"

"A week from this Sunday. It'll be about two o'clock in the afternoon. They'll have a potluck dinner at the church afterward with most of the congregation sending them off for a short honeymoon. They'll be gone for a couple of days."

"I have been invited, but I can't go because I have to

work that Sunday. Unfortunately, the church isn't on my beat, or I could drop in at the dinner for a few minutes to congratulate the kids."

They rode on a while in silence with Carley taking in all the scenery. They passed through Woodstock and turned right onto Stony Creek Road, halfway through Edinburg. After a couple more miles, Terry turned onto a gravel driveway leading up a short hill to the back of a white clapboard house. Chickens scattered and Carley saw a tan cow looking dolefully over a split rail fence. Looking up at the distant mountains she saw shadows scudding across the landscape made by clouds sailing between earth and the bright late July sun high in the sky. She was fascinated by the scene, one she had never seen in her life in the city. Terry followed where her eyes were focused and realized that she was seeing in awe something he had taken for granted all his life.

"Beautiful, isn't it?" I used to love to come out here and lie on my back and watch those clouds and shadows. In fact, I often found the clouds formed rabbits, ducks, and even Mickey Mouse," he grinned.

From across the road a man in grey overalls came toward them. His powerful muscled arms let Carley know this was Terry's blacksmith father.

In confirmation, Terry strode across the yard, putting his arms out for the bear hug he received from the huge grey-haired man.

Terry's mother pushed the kitchen screen door open and stepped down the couple of wood planks serving as outdoor steps to the gravel driveway. She wiped her hands on the

Mother Hubbard apron made from chicken feed-sacks; she put out her hands and clasped Carley's and drew her into a warm hug. Carley, so unused to such a show of affection could only mumble "Thank you, Mrs. Clanahan."

"It's 'Mom'." Agnes Clanahan corrected. Carley looked over at Terry who stood with a silly grin on his face and shrugged his shoulders and looked skyward.

Carley turned just in time to receive another big hug from Dad Clanahan. She resigned herself to the fact she had been blessed with a new family whether she had said 'I do' yet or not.

The kitchen exuded aromas of frying chicken, baking squash and fresh yeast rolls. Still warm zucchini bread rested on the large oak sideboard. A big bowl of coleslaw made with whipped cream was brought from the icebox as they sat down to lunch at the long kitchen table. Before the meal was completely set out, Dad Clanahan opened the front door in the living room to shoo two dogs and three cats outside.

Carley looked around the large room where a huge black Majestic wood stove stood. Its shiny large smoke stack curved through the side wall just under the ceiling. The windows were open and a soft cross breeze pushed out the heat still coming from the earlier cooking.

After the prayer, given by Roger Clanahan, for the food, the cook, and the new litter of piglets courtesy of their sow "Susie", they dove into the food interrupted only by a few "please pass" a dish or two.

Soon, Dad pushed back a bit from the table and turned

to Carley. "Terry tells me you're a wonderful cook. Cook for a household of folks, I understand."

"It's just plain food. No French sauces or pastries. Just plain solid food. I do intend adding Mrs. Clanahan's cole-slaw with whipped cream as a treat once in a while."

"Nothing wrong with that. In fact, I don't think I'd want to eat some of those dishes with snails and such. No, my taster goes more for plain meat and 'taters than snails." He made such a screwed-up face Carley almost choked on a piece of bread roll she had buttered and slathered with rasp-berry jam.

"I promise you, Dad, I'm well fed when I put my legs under her table . . . ." He reached for Carley's hand and she allowed him to hold it momentarily, not wanting to make a big deal out of it, but she surely intended talking to Terry on the way home to get some things straightened out. A few seconds later she withdrew her hand to take her napkin and dab at her lips.

Agnes Clanahan rose from her seat and began to clear the table of the used dishes and Carley began to push away from her place to help.

"Stay seated, Carley. I'm just clearin' away for our des-sert." Agnes put a hand on Carley's shoulder.

"Goodness, I should have saved room. I'm stuffed!" Carley puffed her cheeks out.

"Oh, this will slide down easy," Agnes said, putting dish-es on the sideboard and reaching into the icebox for a big bowl of vanilla pudding. She put a generous serving in each bowl and topped it off with a slice of the zucchini bread Carley had observed before.

Roger pulled back up to the table, obviously pleased with his wife's selection of sweets for the meal. Carley wasn't too sure he was going to say grace again.

"Mother, you've outdone yourself," he said between bites. "This is excellent. Son, when we're done, let's take Carley on a tour of the place. She'll need to walk off all this good food."

"I should stay and help with the dishes," Carley protested.

"Now, you go on ahead. I'll only be a few minutes and then I'll join you. As you can see, the pots and pans are already clean. I always do them up as I go. My mother taught me that."

"Well, okay, if you say so," Carley followed the men out the door.

They first walked down across the road where grassy acreage led to a large fast flowing creek with thick foliage lining each side. Rows of berry bushes cut through several places like dark green fences. A garage was built next to the big hog yard, and Susie came ambling over to the fence, snorting her greeting to her friend who pulled a bread roll from his back pocket and handed it to her. He reached down and rubbed her head with his knuckles.

"Mother doesn't approve of me giving Susie her bread rolls, but we won't tell her, will we?"

"She knows," Terry grinned. "She always has."

Dad Clanahan chuckled. "I guess you're right, son. I guess you're right."

Carley felt the love between the two men and felt a tang of envy. She had never known the love of a father and the love she shared with her mother had been so short lived. There had been no love between Aunt Florence and herself. She felt it a duty to love her grandmother, but after so many years of obvious rejection, she had stopped trying. Her attention was drawn from her inner feelings to some movement in the shadows of the garage where a couple of piglets began to squeal in hunger for their mother. The sow lumbered over to them and lay down, and they noisily nuzzled her climbing over each other to grab onto a tit.

"Oh my," Carley marveled. "I've never seen a live pig before, let alone a mother with her babies. I'd love to hold one of the little ones."

"Oh no." Roger laughed. "I don't touch them unless I've separated Susie from them by putting her out to the pasture. She'd take my leg off if I tried to pick one up while she's around. She's a very protective mother."

"Even though you're the one who feeds her and pets her?" Carley asked.

"You've a lot to learn," Terry put his arm around her waist. "Let's visit Dad's blacksmith shop. It's right beside the garage."

They climbed the slight incline around the side of the pig yard and came to the one lane road that ran past the house, and stepped inside a crude three-sided room. The fourth wall was a door that slid sideways on a rail at the top. The other three walls were covered with deerskins, metal wheels, tools and horseshoes. In the middle of the room was a round heavy metal kettle with ashes piled in the middle. Beside it stood a large anvil, with a huge hammer resting on it.

"Tools, wheels and horseshoes," Terry's arm swept around the room. "And knives, Dad can temper metal to make the sharpest knives. Everyone around here brings their scissors and knives to sharpen."

"Terry's good at it, too." Roger was obviously proud of his son. "But there's not enough work around here for another blacksmith."

Roger pulled the big door closed, and they walked across the road to the ice house, a room dug out of the side of the hill. It was once used as a stable for the cow, but now it was packed with bales of straw insulating large chunks of ice cut from the creek when it was frozen in the winter. It isn't edible but is cheaper than buying ice for the icebox, just to keep the food cool."

They were walking up the driveway toward the chicken houses where they could see Agnes carrying a bag of chicken feed. "I'll have to order a couple blocks of ice next week. Don't tell your mother, but I've been putting some money away to get her a refrigerator for Christmas."

"Can I add to the pot," Terry asked.

"You just bought a car, son."

"Well, that wasn't much and now that I've been mooching off Carley at her dinner table, I've been able to save quite a bit."

"You've been doing what?" Agnes said as she approached them across the yard.

"Your son has been freeloading on his girlfriend, Mother." Roger explained. "But I don't really see her objecting to it."

"It is really comforting, Mrs. Clanahan, to have a policeman in the house especially . . . ," Carley stopped herself from speaking her fears of having a murderer in the midst of her boarders, "especially since I'm quite fond of him."

Agnes was strewing corn on the ground for her chickens and trailed the grain behind the chicken wire fence to entice them back into their yard for the rest of the day."

"It's not every night," Terry protested. "And Carley says she is grateful not to have so many leftovers."

"That's right. I really do like having an officer at the table. No one will steal the silverware."

Roger guffawed and slapped his knee. "That's a good one, Carley, me girl, a good one."

Agnes finished scattering the chicken feed and Roger took a galvanized pail to the pump at the corner of the house, returning to fill the trough for the hens. The hens kept picking at the grain not even moving out of the way of Roger's big boots.

"Kind of greedy, aren't they?" Carley laughed.

"Oh, yes. No table manners at all." Agnes agreed.

"Well, a couple of them will be eating their last meal for they will be a meal Sunday at the church potluck dinner."

"How do you chose which one's?"

"Well, those two big ones will go. The ones we ate at lunch were pullets. About a year old. They were tender fryin' chickens. Those big ones will take stewin' to make them tender, so they'll do very well in the casserole I intend making for Sunday."

"I never thought about why I bought fryers or roasters at the store. I just paid attention to the labels."

"Live and learn," Terry advised. "Wait until Thanksgiving when we butcher the hog. You'll see where a lot of meat choices come from."

"What? One of Susie's babies?" Carley said in disbelief.

"Not this year. We have a hog we're feeding back in a pen over past the smokehouse. He's from last year's litter."

Carley looked like she was ready to cry, but Terry put his arm around her shoulder and gave her a squeeze.

"Cheer up, honey," he soothed, "I have no intention of being a farmer."

Carley felt a bit appeased but also a bit pressured. I'll wait until we're on our way home before I remind Terry I haven't said "yes" yet, she thought to herself.

After the tour was over, Roger and Agnes began filling some paper bags with corn, tomatoes and squash. The next day he would be filling the back of his truck with like produce, along with eggs and butter, to sell to folks without gardens in town who want farm fresh groceries. Agnes would take care of slopping the hogs, feeding the cows and chickens for the day while Roger would be gone.

Carley knew better than to protest the gift of food and gave Agnes a kiss of the cheek along with her thanks.

"That's enough," Terry protested as he walked back from the car where he had placed the bags of vegetables on the back seat.

"Be careful, kids," Roger said as he and Agnes waved to them as they backed out of the driveway. He bent down and gave Agnes a kiss on her forehead as they turned to go back into the shade of the wide porch.

⌒

Carley was silent for a long time before Terry spoke up. "A penny for your thoughts."

"I'm thinking," Carley said seriously, "that you have taken my feelings for granted."

It was Terry's turn to be silent in thought.

"I'm sorry, honey, I guess I did get ahead of things with Mom and Dad. I was just hoping and hoping you would say 'yes'."

He looked so downcast, like a chastised puppy dog, Carley felt sorry for him. But, she thought, Roger and Agnes had been married almost forty years. Horace and Beatrice had been married forty years, and they were visibly still in love.

"Terry" she spoke his name but said nothing more.

"Yes?"

"Oh, nothing. I was just thinking that I never knew what it was like to have a family . . . what a marriage really is . . . you know, a father, mother and kids. I wouldn't know how

I would be expected to act or do. I'm scared at the thought. I just don't know what I'd be expected to do, or if I could even do it." She fell silent after this spate of words and just looked out the window.

"I understand what you mean," Terry said. "I guess most people have those fears. They muddle through, and most get it right. I think the good Lord guides them along if they ask him."

"Give me just a little more time," Carley patted his hand. "Just a little more time."

Twelve

"I'm going to go with Bill to his church this morning," Bucky announced while reaching for the orange marmalade for his toast. "It's the grey stone church on H Street just a couple of blocks away."

Carley smiled. "Your mother will be pleased you've found one. Did you go to a Methodist church in Morgantown?"

"No. We went to a Presbyterian church. Actually, there's a Presbyterian church meeting at this church while their building is being built across the street."

Bucky was dressed in a white shirt and sported a blue four-in-hand tie. His unruly curly hair had been slicked back with pomade. "By the way, Bill, I've been meaning to ask, what do you do all day when you go to work?"

Bill stopped chewing, took a swallow of his juice before answering. "I type manuscripts in Braille from wax cylinders."

"You what?" Eulali asked in amazement.

"Well, you know, it's called transcription. Typists do it in offices, only they use regular typewriters. Some can take down what their boss wants them to write from shorthand notes, I understand."

"Yes," Bucky said, "I've seen them in the school office. Someone talks into a horn-like contraption, and somehow a needle scratches the voice onto the wax. When it's put on another machine, the typist can hear that voice."

"It's Edison's invention, I understand," Bill said. "But sightless people like me can't see what is printed so they need Braille bumps to run their fingers over. So . . . that's what I give them . . . bumps!"

"What an amazing talent you have," Carley smiled at him, knowing he couldn't see her face. "I guess you have to be a very accurate typist."

"Yes, my boss or someone is hired to just read what I type . . . and what two other typists do . . . they read everything. Don't want to brag, but I have received two "Most Accurate" letters in my file at work."

"Congratulations!" Carley exclaimed. "Not to change the subject, but have any of you heard Bill play the grand piano in the ballroom?"

"Not me," Peter turned to face Bill at the table. "You play the piano?" he asked.

Bill blushed. "Only when I think the room is vacant."

"Bill, don't feel that way," Carley chided, "I'm certain they all would like to hear your lovely music. It's really wonderful."

"Please play for us this evening," Eulali said earnestly.

"We'll see," Bill said as Horace stepped into the room.

"Miss Carley, may I ask for a breakfast tray for Beatrice

again this morning? If she doesn't feel much better today, I think I'll call for Dr. Payne tomorrow."

"Why not call today?"

"It's Sunday, and I hate to disturb him on the Sabbath."

"Well, you know best, I suppose," Carley sighed and headed to the kitchen to ask Frances to fix up a tray.

Frances rolled her eyes up to the ceiling. "If she was my wife, I'd not care who got disturbed. Ain't right she not getting help when she needs it."

"Now, Frances, it's not our place to judge his ways."

"Yes'm. Miss Carley. You're right, but it still ain't right."

Carley smiled and walked back into the dining room where a brisk discussion was going on about Bill's wardrobe. Eulali had remarked on Bill's outfits always matching. Even perfectly color coordinated.

"I believe, with all you can do, you are just fooling us," she laughed. Give up! You can see, can't you?"

Bill good-naturedly humphed and took a sip of his coffee, not answering Eulali, but she would not let it go.

"Your jackets and pants always match. Even your shoes are the right ones."

"My, you've been wasting a lot of your time looking at me, haven't you?" Bill laughed.

"Well, it's hard not to, Bill. You're a good-looking guy. And now we find out you're extra talented, too."

"As for the shoes," Bill teased. "Buddy picks them out for me."

Bucky smiled at Eulali, "I'm sure Bill has a system. I've

got a system. I put my things in my dresser drawers so I could dress in the dark if need be."

Eulali didn't seem satisfied, and a heavy thoughtful silence fell on the eating boarders.

Finally, Bill said, "Okay, I'll tell you. It has to do with safety pins."

"Safety pins! Oh, come on," Eulali said in disbelief.

"Yes, safety pins. Once a year my brother, who lives in North Carolina, comes up to visit and goes through all my clothes, making sure they're clean and the pins are in place. You see, one pin in the nape of the neck of a jacket means it is blue, two brown, and three grey. The same goes for the pants in the back. I always wear white shirts for work, and all my oxfords shoes are black. The wingtips are brown. Both the heavy winter and summer weights have the same pin code. It is really simple, you see."

"How ingenuous," Eulali exclaimed.

"My socks are white cotton or black silk. My brother, Larry, came up with the code, I understand, years ago when he caught me wearing some really outlandish combination of colors. I don't think you ever met him. The last time he came was just before you came here. He's due to come back soon, however."

"I'm looking forward to meeting your brother, Bill. I really am. He must be a real fine person to care so much about his brother." With that, Eulali, excused herself and rose from the table. Everyone watched as she bounced out of the room . . . they always did.

Carley was seated at the dining room table when Tillie

came in with some newly ironed napkins she placed on the table.

"Miss Carley," she almost whispered, "Can I disturb you for a moment?"

Sure. What's up?" Carley put down her pencil she had been using to check off figures in her checkbook.

"I just thought I'd ask if I could have the key to the drawers and doors here on the highboy. I've never seen what's in the drawers or the shelves below, and I just thought," she was talking fast and excitedly, "I'd clean them out to use for napkins and serving silver, instead of having to always bring them in from the kitchen each time we used them."

"Sounds like a plan, Tillie. In fact, I don't know what's in them myself. Aunt Florence never showed me and always kept the key on that ring. Let's do it!"

Carley picked out a small key from the same ring that had housed the skeleton key for the ballroom. She handed it to Tillie. "Here, you do the honors. I need to get back to my house bookkeeping." She had barely sat down at the table and picked up her pencil when Tillie came over with a small flat box.

"What's this?" she handed it to Carley.

Carley took the box and examined it. "It's a box of incense."

"What's incense?" Tillie wrinkled her eyebrows.

"Well, when I was a very little girl, incense was a popular way of making a room smell real pretty. Somewhere in there should be an incense burner. Just a little ceramic thing. These are Chinese. People used to like the home to smell nice. I remember Aunt Florence saying mice had died in the walls and incense made the house smell okay."

"How old were you?"

"Just a little girl. Maybe four. Aunt Florence used to use lavender salts in her bath. Made the whole front hall smell good and fresh when she opened the door to the bathroom after she took a bath."

"Mamma uses pretty smelling sachets in her bedroom drawers. Makes her underwear smell fresh and nice. I think Daddy likes to smell them, too. I caught him one day when I was taking some of her ironed clothes to their room. He looked embarrassed, but I just thought it was funny."

Carley smiled and turned her head to her task on the table. In a few short minutes, Tillie pulled out several dress patterns and laid them down in front of Carley.

"Oh my," Carley grinned. "Look how old-fashioned and out-of-date these are. I think my mother used them to make clothes years and years ago. Might as well toss them in the trash."

"Did you ever sew?" Tillie asked her while stacking the patterns on the table.

"No, never did. I just wasn't talented that way."

Tillie cleaned out the drawers of various odds and ends, including a dried-up apple. Carley caught her looking with high eyebrows at the fruit and started laughing.

"Aunt Florence used to hide the best apple out of the bag for herself. More than once she would forget where she had hidden one, and it would just shrivel away."

Tillie was still giggling when she opened the door to the bottom. There on the shelves was a full set of gorgeous china—all blue and white with pretty scenes of trees and flowers and tiny houses with picket fences and gates.

Carley jumped up from the table and went down on her knees to lovingly take a cup in her hands.

"These were my great grandmother's. She used them when very special people came to dine. I think there's a service for sixteen here, if I remember correctly."

"They're just gorgeous," Tillie carefully ran her finger over the edge of a cup. "They fill up the shelves down here. There's no place for anything else."

Carley stood up and as she did she noticed a silverware box on a small shelf near the top of the shelves. She pulled it out carefully and laid it on the table. When she opened it, a full set of sterling silver tableware sparkled up at her from under a cloth of what they called "President's" cloth to keep silver from tarnishing. Carley knew she had a very valuable item in her hands. She pulled out a chair from the table and placed the set upon her lap. She started counting and found she had a service for twenty-four.

"I'll probably never use any of this," she said as she lovingly examined each serving piece and put it back in place, covering them up with the cloth. "Put it back, Tillie. Who knows, the time might come. Maybe," she sounded wistful.

"There's plenty of room," Tillie said "for everyday silver and the napkins in the drawers, once I get rid of the patterns, incense and dried apple cores."

"You do that, and I'll get back to my checkbook."

It wasn't long before Carley began to smell the odd odor of Chinese incense. Frances and Tillie came into the room from the kitchen and put a small burner on the highboy.

"Guess it would smell better than dead mice," Frances said. "Tillie told me what you said Old Missus Mertins used it for," she laughed. "But I can't say I really like it."

"Me, either," Carley agreed. "Probably too old. Let's just throw it out and forget about it.

"Suits me," Tillie agreed as she took it back into the kitchen.

Peter stuck his hand around the corner of the kitchen door jamb and tapped on the wall.

"Next week's fix-up time. I've put in for my vacation, and there's no reason I won't get it. I head for home when my shift ends tomorrow night to pick up the truck and stuff. Why don't you start shopping for the paint and wallpaper, and put them on hold. I'll pick them all up when I get back with the truck."

"Sounds good. I won't have to pay for store delivery. Just park the truck in the back alley when you get back. Can I pay your father for the use of the ladders and brushes?"

"Nope. I already asked. He said it was worth it to see me doing some real honest work for a change," Peter grinned.

"I'm sure he was just joking," Carley smiled.

Peter looked hard at Carley. "No, he isn't joking," he said. "He doesn't think his son has turned out very good. He thinks bus driving is a soft job. Guess I've really disappointed him."

"Oh, Peter, I'm so sorry to hear that. He's making a big mistake. Your job is honorable and very necessary. Not everybody has the ability to do it. He'll come around some day."

"I hope so. Mother kind of cringes every time he brings up the subject. I feel like telling him, if he was such a good provider, Mother wouldn't have to be a seamstress to make ends meet. But I don't . . . it would really make her feel worse if we got into a fight over the subject.

"That's wise," Carley walked over to the stove where a dozen eggs had come to a boil in the large saucepan. She shut off the gas and put a cover over the pan. For lunch she would make egg salad sandwiches with finely chopped celery and paprika and served with barley soup. A bowl of cookie dough stood on the butcher block, as Carley reached for the flour canister, the rolling pin, and the cooker cutter.

"That looks mighty good," Peter almost stuck his finger in the dough but thought better of it. "My mom always let me have a little pinch of the raw dough before she baked it."

Carley laughed, "Well, I'm not your mom. But, if you don't tell anyone, and your hands are clean, go ahead and take a pinch."

Peter did, said "thanks" and disappeared through the dining room and out the front door.

He's such a child, Carley thought, but remembered the blue jay and that day's events and shook her head. Maybe he's the one . . . but maybe not.

⌒

When Frances and Tillie came back downstairs after putting fresh towels and washcloths in the upstairs bedrooms, they were greeted by a large bundle on the dining room table wrapped in white tissue and a large white ribbon with two gold bells. The large tag said simply, "Tillie". Both women were speechless until Carley came in from the kitchen wiping her floury hands on her apron.

"Go on . . . open it. It's for you and your husband-to-be from me."

Tillie held one of the bells in her fingers. "It's so pretty, I hate to tear it up."

"If'n it was mine, I wouldn't hesitate a bit. Go on child, open it up," Frances urged.

With a wide smile flashing across her white even teeth, Tillie carefully pulled the ends of the bow releasing the two bells that tinkled until they rested on the table. Tillie carefully pulled the tissue away to reveal the gorgeous quilt. Tears welled up in her eyes as she looked up at Carley. Frances said, "O my", over and over again as she helped Tillie and Carley unfold the quilt and spread it over the table.

"Can I give you a hug?" Tillie asked with a sheepish grin.

"Of course," Carley laughed and spread her arms wide to receive Tillie's grasp.

"Not too hard," Frances warned. "You forget your strength. She might break and we don't want that!"

"It's the Wedding Ring pattern. When I saw it I could almost swear it had 'Tillie' written on the tag.

"Stan will be so pleased. He has rented a room over a deli near Washington Circle. He has a big double bed, a table, a couple of chairs and a dresser. His folks have given us sheets and pillows and a wool blanket from their house. We have a few dishes we've gotten from soap boxes and that's about all."

"She'll get a lot of things at the wedding. Most folks will bring their gifts to the church." Frances put her arms around her daughter's shoulders.

"Oh, but nothing like this," Tillie took a corner of the quilt and buried her face in it. "Nothin like this." Impulsively, she grabbed Carley and hugged her again. "Thank you. Thank you. Thank you."

"Enough," Carley laughed. "I have cookies in the oven. I hope they're not burnt." She raced to the oven, pulled down the door and found two sheets of golden brown cookies glistening with sprinkled sugar on top. They weren't burned at all, she sighed in relief.

"Thank you, Lord," she looked skyward, "for looking after them when I wasn't." She heard tissue crinkling and soon the ladies came through the door and laid the precious bundle on the third stair, where it would be safe until they were headed home. Carley couldn't help but notice that Tillie often went over and looked at the package the rest of the day, and once she even bent over and patted the white bundle very lovingly.

Thirteen

Sun streamed in the window making crystal cruets on the highboy sparkle with all the colors of the rainbow. The ceiling reflected the same shimmering colors. Everyone except Horace and Beatrice had congregated around the table and a murmur of well-being caressed them.

The coffee refills were being poured when Horace slowly entered the dining room, his eyes red and rimmed with tears. He looked for Carley and took her by the elbow and went back into the hallway. He was wearing a maroon smoking jacket that sagged off his shoulders replicating the sad mood Horace's face showed. "Miss Carley," he choked on the words and then took a deep breath. "Miss Carley, Beatrice has gone."

"Gone?" Carley asked as if she thought the lady had simply left the house. "She passed away during the night. When I woke about a half hour ago, she just lay there beside me with a peaceful smile on her face."

"Oh, Horace. I'm so sorry. I didn't realize she was so ill."

"She had a bad heart. It ran in her family. Her sister, Bonnie, does, too. While Beatrice didn't display the weakness Bonnie does, she had been afflicted for a long time.

I need to call Dr. Payne to come before I can make other arrangements. May I use the phone in the hall? I won't be long."

"Of course, take all the time you need." She turned to go back into the dining hall, and then stopped. "Do you want me to tell the others?"

"Yes, I wish you would. Thank you."

Horace took a large handkerchief out of his jacket pocket and blew his nose and dabbed at his eyes.

Carley left him dialing the phone and slowly stepped back into the breakfast room.

"Frances," she whispered, "Come in the kitchen with me, please."

"What's the matter, Miss Carley, you look like somethin's awful wrong."

"Yes, dear, something sad has happened. Mrs. Owens has passed away in her sleep. Mr. Owens is calling for the doctor and will be making arrangements to have the coroner and undertaker come, I guess."

"That's so sad. They are . . . were . . . such a devoted couple. Is there anything I can do?"

"Yes, I want you to fix up a tray with extra coffee on it for Mr. Owens, and take it up to his room . . . or have Tillie take it up."

"Oh, no mam's," Tillie, who had overheard the news, said quickly. "I'm not going into any room with a dead body in it. Not me!"

"Don't be silly," Frances smiled at her daughter. "But don't worry, I'll take it up."

Carley slowly walked back into the dining room and rested her hands on the back of her chair. She lowered her head in a silent prayer for the right words to say.

"I need your attention, folks. Horace has just told me that Beatrice passed away during the night. He woke up and found her passed. He wanted me to tell you all that I didn't know she had been ill, but he says she has been for quite a while. There will be a lot of coming and going, I guess, for a couple of days, and I'll let you know what kind of arrangements he makes when he tells me."

"Is there anything we can do?" Eulali asked. Carley saw tears in her eyes. Eulali had always been so carefree and flip. Her tears were a surprise.

"Nothing yet that I know of," Carley sat down at the table and picked up her coffee cup, and Tillie immediately filled it for her. The room fell into silence.

Two deaths in Mertins Manor in as many months. Things are getting a bit spooky around here, Carley thought. A slight chill gripped her even though the late July heat shimmered outside the window.

⌒

"Frances, please help me pull that heavy armoire out of my bedroom into the hall. I'll use it for my clothes and bedding while Peter is painting and papering my room. And find those two large oscillating fans to put in there to air out the room. I think they're in the attic."

"Yes ma'am." Frances smiled as she turned to get Tillie. The door chimes rang, they heard Tillie answer and open the door to the funeral home director dressed in somber black.

Tillie directed him up the steps to the room on the second floor and then came back down into the hallway. It wasn't long before the man came back down and opened the door to two gentlemen pulling a wheeled gurney into the house.

Carley was glad everyone else had either gone to work or was staying in their rooms. It took only a short time until the hallway was again silent as she heard the hearse, which had been parked at the curb on 18th Street, pull away and merge into other traffic.

Carley, Frances and Tillie stood and looked at each other and then turned their attention to the chore at hand, rolling the heavy chifferobe into the hallway on its small metal and wood casters.

Carley selected several dresses, slips and other underwear, and put them on one side of the big shelf and closed the door. Then, she put a couple of sheets and her big feather pillow on the floor of the mobile closet, along with her slippers, robe and nightgown.

"There," she said aloud, "That should be enough for the week it will take Peter to get the job done."

"I can hardly wait," Tillie grinned. "Are you going to do over all the rooms?"

"Not right now, but maybe I'll do some of the others when they get vacant before getting a new tenant. I hadn't really thought about that, but you're right. Almost all the rooms are a bit shabby. Depends on the money, girls."

"What happened," Terry's voice echoed down the hallway. "I saw the hearse leave the curb out front. Was it for here?"

"Yes," Carley beckoned for him to come into the kitchen and reached for the coffee pot and a cup from the cabinet. "Beatrice Owens passed away this morning, or I should say, sometime during the night."

"I didn't think she was sick enough to die. Frail, perhaps, but not really ill."

"She had a bad heart and, evidently, she died during the night. She was gone when Horace awoke this morning."

"Real sorry to hear that."

"He's up in his room, I think. Don't go up. I think he'll probably be down for dinner. In the meantime, I have to go downtown to buy my paint and wallpaper. Want to go along?"

"Sure. I'm off my shift right now. I'm doing a split. They want me downtown about ten. There's going to be some kind of speech-making down in shantytown. Might get a bit out of hand, especially if there's too much drinking.

"Oh my, please be careful." Carley said with fear in her voice.

"I'm always careful, my dear. Always."

"Frances," Carley turned her attention to her kitchen help. "Put out sandwich meat and potato salad for lunch. Mr. Wampler is at work. Bucky and Miss West will probably be here. I haven't seen Mr. Foucher, and I don't know if Mr. Owens will come down. I shouldn't be long. Tonight's dinner is already in the refrigerator to be heated up."

Carley picked up her pocket book and went out the front door, followed by Terry. They walked slowly down the brick street to the corner and crossed over heading to the White

House on Pennsylvania Avenue. Soon, they were on busy shop-lined G Street. Big department stores were on each side of the broad streets reaching high in the sky; making one side in cool shadow. They entered the quiet store where chairs circled tables filled with wallpaper sample books. Carley quickly found the lovely pink roses on a trellis she had seen before and purchased what she needed, setting it aside for later pickup. The paint was sold in the back of the store, and again, she quickly found what she wanted, paid for it and had it set aside. She and Peter would pick it up when he got back from his Dad's place in a couple of days.

"You know, Terry," Carley said over a malt at the drugstore counter, "I had a real cold feeling when Horace told me Beatrice was dead. That's two deaths in my house in just a few weeks."

"Now, don't tell me you think this is a suspicious death, too." Terry chided.

"I don't know what to think. Don't laugh at me."

"I'm not laughing, honey. I have to admit it does seem strange. But it's probably just all a sad coincidence."

"Maybe. Maybe," Carley murmured as she took a final sip of her drink. "Maybe."

Fourteen

Dreams of the deaths of Aunt Florence and Beatrice had disturbed Carley's sleep, and she woke early in a cold sweat. Throwing on her robe, she quietly went into the kitchen and put on the coffee pot. She stepped out the back door and realized the sun had just barely risen past the treetops. It was just a little past five in the morning. Sitting quietly on the iron bench which was covered with light morning dew, she closed her eyes and prayed for peace of mind. After a few minutes she took a deep breath, looked skyward and felt a load lift off her bent shoulders. Smiling, she rose and headed back to the kitchen where the percolator had finished its job and poured herself her first cup of coffee for the day.

Carley walked into her bathroom and drew a lukewarm bath liberally spiked with lavender salts. She took a deep breath and stepped into the large freestanding iron tub with eagle claw and ball feet.

She sank in up to her shoulders, and it took all her reserve not to slip back to sleep.

By the time she had finished her bath, it was getting close to time for Frances and Tillie to arrive. She dressed quickly and was soon putting napkins and silverware on the table.

Horace came into the room and the ladies could hear murmurs of sympathy as each of the other boarders entered.

"I guess you all would like to know my arrangements for the funeral. Beatrice's early family had grave plots in Cumberland, Maryland. The cemetery is behind the All Soul's Church. The service will probably be Saturday. I'll understand if you can't come. It's a long trip there. In fact, I'll be staying with friends there for a couple of days myself."

He had said it all as though practiced, which, of course, it was. Except for a couple nods of heads or murmurs, there was no immediate response as each boarder considered their options.

"Let us know where flowers can be sent." Carley said, breaking the silence. Murmurs of agreement came from around the table.

The rest of breakfast was muted, and soon the room was empty and dishes were being washed.

Carley sighed as if the whole morning had been an ordeal, and she was glad it was over. She hadn't realized how apprehensive she had been over this first meal with Horace present.

Before she had a chance to really relax with all the morning chores done, Tillie came rushing into the room, a look of disbelief on her face.

"Miss Carley! Miss Carley! "She almost shouted. "I just came from the ballroom, and someone has stolen that little statute on the mantel next to the front windows. You know, the little French dandy holding a bird on his finger. It's gone!"

"Now, calm down, Tillie. It's nothing to get yourself in an uproar about. First, it's not a very valuable statute, I don't think."

"Well, maybe, but somebody took it, and it doesn't belong to them. They stole it!"

Carley rested her chin on her hand, deep in thought. A smile crossed over her lips as she looked Tillie in the face.

"I think I know who has it."

"Who?" Tillie sat down across the table and looked Carley in the eyes.

"Do you remember that day when we were standing in the hallway and Mr. Foucher came down and dropped all those canvas paintings?"

"Yes, I remember."

"Well, one of them was a still life and had that vase in the den on the reading table. He had borrowed it to use for his still life painting, and had then returned it. I bet it won't be long before you'll find the little figurine back on the mantel, too. Let's not say anything about it to anyone and just bide our time. If it doesn't reappear, then we'll have to worry if we do, indeed, have a thief among us."

And a murderer, as well, Carley thought, and again a chill went down her back between her shoulder blades.

Oogah! Oogah! The raucous sound of the old Model T truck blared from the back alley announcing Peter's arrival. Carley raced across the yard and swung the two gates wide so he could drive in toward the house.

"Stop and get some refreshment before you start unloading. Some of that big pile of canvas and ladders will probably have to go in the cellar until you are ready to use them. We'll figure that out later though. Come on in."

Peter stepped down from the running board, wiping his brow with a large red handkerchief.

"A little refreshment sounds good. I only stopped for gas and a Coke along the way. Want to get started soon as I can."

"Go over to the sink there and wash your face with cold water. There are clean towels on the shelf below. I'll fix you a sandwich and pour you a tall glass of lemonade. That's what we had at lunch."

"Sounds wonderful," Peter said sloshing cold water over his face and then sticking his head under the faucet to wet his sweaty hair.

Carley sat down at the table and poured two glasses of lemonade, telling him about Beatrice and all that had happened since he had gone.

"I didn't think she was really ill at all. She walked those four long blocks to her sister's place every morning. If she was so sick, she couldn't have done that, could she?"

"A bad heart lets you do a lot sometimes, and then it just gives out, I guess."

"Has Horace said anything about burial arrangements?"

"Yes, he told us at breakfast yesterday, but I don't think anyone can go. It's to be in Cumberland; awfully far away."

"Yes, it is. I never knew where she was from," Peter said between gulps of lemonade and bites of the sandwich Carley set in front of him.

"Soon as you get done," Carley said, "we'd better get the truck emptied. I heard a rumble of thunder a minute ago. No need to get all your equipment wet. I'll help carry in the brushes and drop cloths."

"Okay. Did you buy all your paint and other supplies?"

"Yes. It's waiting for us to pick it up at the store anytime."

"Why don't you just give me the paperwork, and I'll pick it up?"

"Not a bad idea," Carley went to her purse and gave him the slips for pickup.

Peter looked over them. "I don't see wallpaper paste here."

"Oh, I forgot about that. They didn't remind me."

"I'll pick up some, so don't worry about the cost. Let's just get this stuff out of the truck before it rains."

Carley started across the yard as Frances and Tillie came running to help. Peter took two short ladders to the cellar door and ran back for a couple baskets filled with paint rags.

"I'll put these down in the cellar. I won't need them until I begin the trim. Did you know there's a plank missing from your cellar door?"

"Yes. It's been missing for quite some time. Aunt Florence never replaced it. The floor down there is only packed down dirt, so the rain can't hurt anything."

"I'll replace it later anyway," Peter said as he lugged the ladders and buckets to the top of the steps.

The three ladies had just finished placing their armloads on the floor of the bedroom when they were shocked by a loud scream and cursing.

"I ought to kill you all, Peter yelled over his shoulder as he opened the screen door to the kitchen, red bloody scratches on the back of his hand.

"What happened?" All three ladies asked in unison.

"Sorry," Peter blushed. "There's a mother cat down in the cellar with six kittens in a basket filled with rags. I guess she went through the gap in the cellar door. I reached down to pick one of the little kittens up, and mamma hissed at me and clawed my hand."

"My," Frances laughed, "You sure do have trouble with Mother Nature."

"Get the iodine," Carley smiled. "They don't look like deep scratches, but we'd better disinfect them anyway."

"I'll still go to the store to get the paint and wallpaper. I'll put the paper in the cab with me so it won't get wet."

"It will be too late to start painting, so you can relax a bit before dinner. I want to go down to see the kittens after that." Carley smiled in expectation. "I love kittens, but Aunt Florence never let me have one."

"Is she an orange stripped cat?" Frances asked.

"Yes'm. But the kittens are all sorts of colors and spots." Peter looked at his hand and shook his head. "But I bet they all have claws."

"That cat belongs to somebody in the neighborhood. I've fed her bits of leftover food, and I knew she was expecting babies. Don't know who she belongs to though." Frances said, putting the disinfectant back in the medicine cabinet.

Peter left in the slick, black truck as Carley turned her attention to the sweet potatoes, washing and buttering them for the oven. She pulled a shank of ham from the refrigerator and sliced off a big plate of ham. Coleslaw finished off the meal, with iced tea and bread rolls she had made the day before and put in the oak pie safe. The pie safe was a heavy oak piece with copper door inserts that had been punched with an awl to make roosters as decoration. As a child, she hardly ever passed it without trailing her fingers over the cool copper birds.

"When it stops raining, Frances," Carley gave her a dollar bill, "go around the corner to High's and get a gallon of Neapolitan ice cream for dessert."

"My, that sounds wonderful," Tillie grinned.

"By the way. How are the wedding plans coming along. It's less than a week away, isn't it?"

"Just fine," Frances replied. "How's Sunday lunch gonna be served?"

"Don't worry. Horace will be at Bonnie's. Eulali will eat at the theatre. Peter is going to fix himself and Bill something from the fridge, and both Bucky and I will be at the church. It's all taken care of."

"Thank you. I was kinda worried about that, and I'd have tried to squeeze lunch in if I had to. Both Mr. Wampler and Mr. Keller are invited. I hope they come."

"By the way, Tillie, you have a week off with pay. Your mother will be doing double duty, I guess, with me. But enjoy your first week of wedded bliss."

Tears came to Tillie's eyes but her wide grin told Carley how pleased she was.

⌒

Before going to bed, Carley stepped into her bedroom to find Peter had spread drop cloths over everything and had set up the tall ladders, ready for his first day's labor. She backed out and retrieved her nightgown, robe, slippers, pillow and sheets from the chifferobe.

Going into the vacant ballroom, she locked the door behind her and made up the Chesterfield couch with the sheets and an afghan that was always draped over the Morris chair. Walking to the tall windows, she looked out over the almost empty street, lit by several streetlights. Shutting the large shutters, she stepped out of her dress and folded it neatly, placing it on the table. She pulled on her gown, slipped between the sheets and reached up to turn off the end table light.

Memories of childhood swarmed in her mind as she remembered early days when she slept here, when Aunt

Florence had rented out all the rooms during tourist season. She did recall the musty smell the room used to have when it hadn't been open for daily use. Tonight it had a bit of smoky aroma for both Horace and Peter smoked pipes.

Smiling, she was almost asleep when she heard someone in the hall. Her head jerked up when someone tried to open the locked door. Whoever it was rattled the knob twice, and then left quietly, evidently making certain he or she was not heard leaving.

Shaken, Carley was now wide awake, and even the scene of Peter and the cats brought some apprehension to mind. My, he does have a terrible temper, she thought. She finally dozed off thinking she would go look at the kittens in the morning.

Fifteen

The shrill whistle of the postman, who put letters into the black mailbox hanging beside the front door, drew Carley to the front of the house. She retrieved several letters and turned back into the hall to confront Wilbur Foucher walking across the hall carrying the missing statuette in his hands.

"Oh, Miss Carley," he flustered, "I didn't see you at the door."

Carley laughed, "Just picking up the mail. What have you there?" she indicated the small figurine by pointing the letters at it. Wilbur turned red in the face and held the porcelain figurine up.

"I borrowed it to paint into a still life. Folks seem to like them and I sell a lot of them."

"Why didn't you just ask me if you wanted to do that?"

"Well, I had asked Mrs. Mertins a long time ago, and she emphatically said 'No'. I won't use her real words. Said I'd probably smash them to bits. I'm really careful, you know."

"I saw the picture you painted with the vase from the

library. It was beautiful."

"I tried to get this put back last night, but the door was locked to the ballroom."

"Oh, so that was you?" Carley exclaimed, laughing. "I had just dozed off when you rattled the knob."

"You were in the room?" Wilbur asked.

"Yes, I'll be sleeping there until Peter gets my bedroom painted and papered. I couldn't sleep with all that odor."

"Probably wouldn't be good for you, either."

"Well, any time you want to borrow anything just let me, Frances or Tillie know. By the way, Tillie had already reported the missing piece, but somehow I knew you had it to paint into one of your still life pictures".

"Thank you, Miss Carley," Wilbur went into the ballroom and came back out with the rose crusted dish that had been sitting on the top shelf of the mirrored étagère.

Carley smiled at him and looked down at the handful of letters. There was the weekly letter for Bucky from his mother and a bumpy letter for Bill from his brother, who was able to use a Braille grid to write letters. Several letters were addressed to Horace, some of them obviously sympathy cards. A couple of them were from his insurance company. He was due back the day after next, so Carley asked Frances to place them on his desk in his room.

Carley chuckled to herself, thinking about how contrite Wilbur had been. She again eliminated him as a suspect. Much too nice.

～

Carley stepped into her bedroom and put her hand to her nose. Fumes from paint assailed her nostrils and stung her eyes.

"Hey, there," Peter called, "grab one of those damp face masks and put it on. I wear one all the time, and I'm used to the smell. It's better when it's damp."

"I was wondering how you could work in these fumes. My, that ceiling looks good. It's so light! Already the room seems bigger."

"I'm ready to do the cornice work. Takes a little more time. Do you want it ceiling white or trim tan?"

"Let's keep it ceiling white. It'll keep the feeling of more space. The tan would draw it in like a frame."

"I agree. I bought semi-gloss white for it at the store so we're fine." Peter turned back to the job. Carley went back into the kitchen and started slicing Grimes Golden applies into two waiting pie crusts. She smiled to herself; for she was satisfied Peter was doing a professional job.

When Bucky came into the dining room for dinner, his arm was around Bill's shoulder, and both men had silly grins on their faces. They sat down silently, but Peter's curiosity for their obvious conspiratorial look had to be satisfied.

"What's up, guys?"

"What do you mean?" Bucky asked breaking into a broad grin.

"You both look like the cat that ate the canary."

"Maybe we did," Bill chuckled. "Maybe we did."

"Come on, now. Fess up. What are you two up to?"

Bucky laughed. "No big secret. Bill and I are going to the burley-que this evening."

"You are what?" Carley asked in open astonishment.

"Going to the Gayety. Eulali gave us passes and we're going to go tonight. I've been several times, and told Bill about it and he'd like to see or, rather, experience it for himself."

"Perhaps I can't see the performers, but I can hear the music and comedy. It'll be new to me and should be fun."

Carley turned her eyes toward the ceiling and gave silent thanks she had not promised Mrs. Keller she would look after Bucky. She guessed no real harm could come from a little racy jokes and some suggestive dancing in scant costumes. "Or could it?" She mumbled softly, shaking her head.

Wilbur had almost choked on his tea at the announcement, and he looked flustered and embarrassed.

"Oh, come on, Mr. Foucher," Bucky said. "Next month I'll get you tickets, too."

Wilbur looked up from his plate. "No, thanks. I know you will think me a prude, but I made a promise to my wife on her death bed to keep away from temptations."

"I didn't know you had been married," Bill exclaimed. "How long has it been since she passed?"

"It's been almost seven years. She was a very devout woman. A saint."

The conversation became muted as they finished their

meal. Carley thought, "Well, I wanted to get to know my boarders. I'm learning a lot . . . some of it I'd rather not know . . . like Peter's temper."

That reminded her of the kittens in the cellar. "By the way, Peter, I went down to see the kittens, but they're gone."

"Guess mamma cat moved them to a safer place where no one will bother them."

"Sounds like she's a good mother," Eulali said. "Yes, a very good mom."

A rare early August breeze wafted over the garden where Carley and Terry sat under the large maple tree next to the roses. It was early evening, and the sun was just beginning to dip behind the buildings to the west. A citronella candle burned, sending its pungent odor as a warning to the mosquitoes to stay away.

"You're still not wearing the ring," Terry pouted.

"I'm really thinking about it. I've had so much on my mind with the redecorating and the wedding tomorrow. I promise it won't be long before I make up my mind. There just seems to be something nagging at me."

"Anything I can help you with?"

"No, but when I solve the puzzle, you'll be the first to know. Please be patient."

Terry stretched his legs out in front of him and leaned back in his chair. They had brought glasses of iced tea out, and he sipped his slowly, deep in thought.

"Have you come to any conclusion as to Aunt Florence's

death?" Carley asked.

"No. I haven't. And I've really given it a great deal of thought."

"Well, besides Peter's terrible temper, I'm stumped, too. But I still don't think it was an accident."

"I'm going to get me a stubborn woman, aren't I?" Terry laughed. "Are you sure you're not at least part Irish?"

"I don't know what I am. Maybe that's part of my problem."

Carley then told Terry about where Bucky and Bill were, and he got quite a laugh out of the thought of a blind man attending a girly show.

"It'll be interesting to hear about it at the breakfast table tomorrow morning." Carley almost giggled. "By the way, remember, Tillie gets married tomorrow afternoon."

"I wish I could go, but I'm on duty." A strong breeze sent a pungent odor of Citronella their way, and Carley rose and took Terry's empty glass from him and started toward the house.

"I've a couple of things to do before turning in, so I guess we'd better say goodnight."

Terry took advantage of the fact both of her hands were full and wrapped his arms around her and kissed her slowly on the lips.

"If my hands were free," Carley teased, "I'd slap your face."

"I know," Terry grinned and then kissed her again.

Sixteen

B reakfast conversation immediately took on a jovial air as Bill and Bucky recounted the events of the night before. Bill was so animated that Buddy kept looking up at his master quizzically.

"The music was wonderful. I've never heard such uplifting strains . . . except, of course, at a revival meeting when I was just a youngster."

"From what I'm hearing," Carley quipped, "It was far from a revival meeting. You'd both better be going to church with me this morning."

"Oh, we intend to go," Bucky smiled. "I'd never miss the chance to get forgiven for some of the thoughts I had last night."

"Eulali, aren't you ashamed, leading these righteous young men astray?" Horace asked.

"I wouldn't say I was the one that led them. I just gave them the opportunity. I didn't take them by the arm!"

"Sure you did. You dragged us kicking and screaming all the way," Bucky teased.

"Tell me, Bill," Carley asked. "Tell me how you saw the show in your mind's eye."

"Well, there was a wonderful aroma in the place. Like excitement. I could feel the motion on the stage. Bucky described the surroundings and the curtains, and I felt the warmth in the air with the music. And the comedians were so funny. Sure, a couple of the jokes were pretty raunchy, but not too much. I guess they were not appropriate if ladies were present, but I could even hear the women in the audience laugh."

"I'm glad you had a good time," Carley stood and began clearing the table. Both Frances and Tillie had been excused, so she had to take care of the chores.

"Let me help," Bucky said, rising and picking up his own plate and cup. "I'm used to this at home."

"Thank you," Carley smiled. He was, she decided such a nice young man. I'm glad, she thought, he's not on my suspect list.

⌒

Carley had taken the streetcar up the avenue and had walked a couple of blocks to reach Frances' church. The wedding was to take place right after the morning service with the lunch reception in the fellowship hall right after. A man dressed in a tan suit, wearing white gloves, met her at the top of the cement stairs and gave her a paper listing the schedule of events.

Inside, Carley found the pews pretty much packed. Bright colorful hats bobbed in every direction. How festive, she thought and smiled, sitting down at a pew near the rear.

She was immediately welcomed by her seated neighbors, and Carley felt right at home. The music swung from the choir behind the pulpit in a rhythm so upbeat Carley could not help but move her feet and shoulders in response.

Carley noted that Bucky and Bill were seated almost halfway down across the aisle with Buddy at Bill's feet. The pew was too crowded for her to join them.

As the last strains of the last hymn floated toward the ceiling, the pastor raised his voice to announce the wedding.

"You are all invited to the wedding of Stanley Lincoln and Tillie Jones. After the wedding, you are invited down to the fellowship hall for refreshments. Makes no matter if you didn't know and didn't bring something to eat. There's more than plenty. The Lord has provided."

Time was allowed for all who wanted to leave to do so, and then the organist played "I Love You Truly" as Stan Lincoln and his Best Man stood looking down the aisle as Tillie, on the arm of Jolie, slowly stepped toward them.

Tillie was wearing a white ankle-length dress, and her face was covered with a white veil under a tiara of daisies. She carried a small white prayer book in her hands with a spray of white daisies. Jolie looked down at his daughter with pride, stepped back after saying, "Her mother and I do." When the pastor asked, "Who gives this woman to be married?"

As he put Tillies hand into Stan's, a ray of afternoon sun streamed through the strained glass window behind the altar and lit the scene.

Carley thought, a blessing. A true blessing.

After a beautiful and meaningful service, the couple, now pronounced man and wife by the pastor, almost ran back down the aisle and through the double doors and down the stairs at the end of the hall. Frances and Jolie and Mr. and Mrs. Lincoln followed to stand in line at the entrance of the huge fellowship hall where the tables, almost creaking with all sorts of meat plates, casseroles, and drinks, lined the left wall. Tables and chairs filled the center, and on the right wall a long table with a three-tiered white cake was surrounded by gifts. Carley saw the wedding ring quilt spread out over a chair sitting by the table and smiled. Most gifts were still wrapped, but Carley saw a couple of salt and pepper shakers, and a clock had been opened and displayed. She imagined most presents would be pretty practical.

A scream and commotion toward the door got everyone's attention, and Carley followed the crowd to see a lady lying at the bottom of the stairs. People were helping her to stand, and as Carley looked up the steps, she saw Jolie standing there, with an inscrutable look on his face. He started down the steps and bent to pick up something. When he reached the bottom, he handed the object to the lady who had fallen.

"Here's your shoe heel," he said, "I guess it broke off and threw you. Are you all right?"

"I'll probably have a couple of bruises, but except for that and being terribly embarrassed, I guess I'll be fine." She looked down at her foot and reached down to pull off both her shoes. "I'll have to go barefoot the rest of the day. Hope no one will mind." She put the shoes and offending heel on a little table holding a vase of flowers and walked into the hall. A sigh of relief swept the onlookers as a couple of low laughs were heard.

Carley couldn't get over her first thoughts of seeing Jolie at the top of those stairs. Could he have been the one who pushed Aunt Florence? Had he been in the house? Of course, I wasn't there, Carley thought, but he certainly had plenty of reasons to hold a grudge against grandmother, if not for himself . . . for his wife and child. This is a joyful wedding, not a funeral, she thought. Carley shook her head to clear it of all negative thoughts and stepped up to get a plate of food from the tables.

⌒

"You are getting paranoid about this," Terry said when Carley had told him about the thoughts she had had when she saw Jolie at the top of the steps.

"Yes, I know," she agreed, "but I can't seem to help myself. I wasn't there, and it's no fun being this way. When I try to just dismiss the whole situation from my mind, it pushes its way back every time I see someone who could have done it. I'm sorry."

"I won't give up on it, honey, but we need to step back a bit and take a deep breath, or you'll be turning this into one of Eulali's nightmares for yourself."

Carley smiled. "I'll try. I really will. I've eliminated a couple. Bill and Wilbur."

"Okay. That's a step. Why them?"

"Wilbur is just too sweet and bashful. He wouldn't hurt a fly. As for Bill, except for the front stairs, I've never seen him on any of the others. At the wedding, he went out and around the building to enter the fellowship hall through a ground floor door, instead of using the stairs which the lady who fell had done."

"Well, let's forget about it this evening. The dinner was excellent, and I'm full and the sky outside has cleared. Let's go sit under the stars and look at the moon. That's what Young Lovers are supposed to do, isn't it?"

Carley rose from the table, walked around Terry's chair and took his hand, and he rose, and they walked arm in arm to the bench under the maple tree.

"I'm going to make a sign for this bench," Terry laughed. "It'll read, 'Lover's Dream Seat'."

Seventeen

rances' scream and gasp, followed by her loud laughter, and Peter's laugh, almost a whoop, made Carley wonder whether she should go into her bedroom or the backyard. The last time she had seen Peter was when he disappeared into her room after breakfast.

Stepping out the back door, she saw a wall of English ivy lying on the ground at Frances' feet.

"What on earth happened?" she pointed to the green vine.

"Mr. Roberts done come through the wall and . . ." She didn't finish her explanation, because Peter stepped over to Carley with a big grin on his face.

"I knew it! I knew it! This old house has lots of history in it. I was sanding the cedar in your closet to liven up the aroma. Wanted to get that done before painting the trim— you know, get all that dust out of the way."

"Yes, yes," Carley said impatiently. "What does that have to do with this situation?" She spread her hands and arms out over the fallen dark glossy green ivy.

Peter took a deep breath to control his excitement. "When I was sanding the cedar, I came across a couple of tiny hinges in the back of your closet. I felt all around the perimeter to see if there was a doorknob of sorts, for where there are hinges . . . the panel must open somehow."

"And did you find a doorknob?"

"No, but I did find a small square of wood opposite the hinges that moved when I pushed it. I did, and the whole back of your closet opened outward."

"And pushed the ivy off the wall!" Frances said, wonder in her voice.

"No, not quite. It opened into a tiny room just big enough to stand or crouch in. I then found another door, and when I pushed it open, the ivy fell."

"Why on earth was there a tiny room in the back of my closet?"

"I think this house was used before the Civil War to hide slaves on their way north."

"I've heard of that," Frances said. "They called it something like a train from the South."

"The 'Underground Railroad'," Carley agreed.

"I'll take the inner door off, if you want, Miss Carley. It'll make your closet almost twice as big."

"Let me think about that, Peter. I guess it's part of history. But I could use the space."

"I can store the door somewhere and if, in the future, you want it put back, it won't be any trouble."

"Let's do that." Carley agreed.

Frances smiled. "My great, great granddaddy was a slave and went north. Maybe he was in there once."

"One never knows," Carley smiled. "One never knows." Then she added to herself, "No, one never knows a lot of things."

Breakfast chatter was exceptionally bright as the secret door was discussed. Terry had also joined the group for coffee, as he didn't need to start his beat until ten o'clock.

"You can use it to sneak in a boyfriend with no one knowing it," Eulali laughed.

"Only you would think of that," Peter grinned.

"Hey," Terry said, "Carley only has one beau, and that's me."

"Hey, Mr. Foucher, maybe you can paint a nice picture for Terry and Miss Carley as a wedding present." Bucky suggested.

Terry laughed. "That's a wonderful idea."

"Remember, I haven't said 'yes' yet." Carley reminded him.

"But you will," Terry teased. "You will. You can't resist my good looks!"

"Don't ask me," Eulali grinned, "if you do, I'll say 'yes', and get you to the altar before you have a chance to take another breath."

Terry, his face brightened, turned to Wilbur, "Wilbur, I am going down to my folks place the third week of September to help with the haying and gathering the last of the garden into the house for Mom to put up in jars for the winter. Why don't you come with me? The scenery that time of the year is gorgeous. The maple trees are turning color."

"I wouldn't want to impose on your folks, Terry," Wilbur said quietly.

"They would love it. My mom wouldn't pass up any chance to feed someone who would appreciate her good cooking. So it's set."

Eulali was flashing a beautiful ruby ring no one had seen before. Finally, Bucky realized the ring was new.

"Where'd you get that hunk of glass, Eulali?"

"Thought you'd never ask." Eulali quipped. "My birthday was yesterday, and the guys and gals down at the theatre threw me a bash. This ring is what they gave me. Ain't it purty?"

"Is that a real ruby?" Horace asked. "If it is, you should insure it against theft."

"No, it's glass but a real good grade. Don't make no difference to me. It's just that they all thought enough about me to get it for me."

I didn't know it was your birthday, or I would have baked a cake for you." Carley said, disappointed.

"That's okay. I don't advertise my years, and I don't know how they knew."

Tillie left to the kitchen to answer the phone that had interrupted the conversation.

"It's for Mr. Owens," she announced at the kitchen door.

"I'll take it on the hall extension." Horace rose from the table and walked into the hall and took the phone on the table. His conversation was low, and he slowly hung up and shuffled into the dining room, his head hung low in dejection.

"That was George, my brother-in-law. He told me Bonnie died during the night."

Carley gasped. "She died?"

"It's not unusual for a twin as close as she and Beatrice had been all their lives to die very close to one another. I've read about it . . . kind of studied twins, after I realized the woman I was going to ask to be my wife was a twin. It's not unusual at all."

"I'm so sorry, Horace. I know how close you two were. Please give my sympathies to George and Janet when you see them."

"I will. I'm going over there now." Horace stepped through the door, leaving a once jolly breakfast group in silent contemplation.

⌒

Peter was absent at the breakfast table. He had left the day before to take the truck and painting supplies back to his dad. He planned on being back in time for dinner.

Carley planned on getting her newly refurbished room back in order. Just the thought made her smile. She could hardly wait for the meal to be over with.

"Welcome back, Tillie," Eulali chirped at the new bride as she came through the door with a pot of coffee in her hands.

"Thank you, Miss West," Tillie beamed.

"I'm sorry I missed your wedding, Tillie," Horace smiled.

"I understand, Mr. Owens. Give my regards to your brother-in-law, please."

"I will. I will." Horace held up his cup to be refilled.

"I'm real happy to have Tillie back. We got along pretty well, but she was certainly missed," Carley said.

"How's married life going?" Eulali asked.

"Just fine, Miss West," Tillie blushed. "Just fine."

Carley stepped into her bedroom as her eyes swept from ceiling and doors, to the walls and window, then back to the doors. Frances had followed her in; Carley heard her "oohing" and "ahhing".

"My, Miss Carley, the room looks twice as big as it did, doesn't it?"

"Yes, it does. It even smells different. No longer musty."

The paint smell had been dispersed by the fans, but Carley had placed lavender sachets in the dresser drawers, and burned some incense in little glass dishes anyway.

Eighteen

Everyone had shown up for breakfast, including Peter in his uniform ready to go back to work on his sight-seeing route. The dishes had been done, and Carley had put the stew beef in the large iron stew pot to simmer. She would add potatoes, carrots, onions and peas later.

"I wish I had asked Peter to help move the chifferobe back into the bedroom before he left," Carley said. I'll have to wait until he gets home, I guess."

"Me and Tillie can move it," Frances volunteered.

"Are you sure. It's awfully heavy you know. Pushing it out wasn't so bad. But we did hit the door jamb a couple of times."

"We'll take it nice and easy; it won't take long."

"Okay," Carley agreed tenuously, "I do want to get my room back in order today. I'm tired of sleeping on the couch in the ballroom."

It wasn't long before all three were standing in the center of the newly painted and wallpapered room looking at the bundles laid out on the bed. Opening one, Carley handed Tillie two shear white curtains for one window.

"You'll have to stand on the cedar chest to reach the top

of that window, Tillie. Please be careful. I wouldn't want you to fall."

"I'll be careful. I'll take off my shoes. Wouldn't want to scar the chest."

Tillie carefully reached up and soon the curtains were billowing in as a breeze wafted in the open window. Then Tillie draped a deep rose valance across the top and stepped down to admire her work.

"One down," Carley said clearly approving Tillie's accomplishment. She handed her another set for the other window. Tillie would have to stand on the desk this time so Carley moved several items from the top to the chair.

A pile of clothes, most still on wire hangers, lay on the bed, and Carley started hanging them in the freshly sanded cedar closet.

"My, but that sure does smell good," Frances exclaimed. "And look at all the extra room you have since Mr. Roberts found that tiny room in the back."

"My clothes rod goes from front to back now instead of across, and he put in a couple narrow shelves. They'll really come in handy."

"He's missing his calling driving that bus around," Frances said.

"Well, he feels he can make a lot more money driving. Not many people need carpenters these days. At least they don't have the money to keep a man busy enough to make a living at it. When times get better, he'll probably go into business with his Dad."

Tillie was really curious about the large bundle on the bed. She lifted it and turned to Carley.

"Can I open this?" she asked.

Carley was tempted to say, "May I?" but thought Tillie might not think the correction very funny. She'd probably take it to heart, Carley thought; don't want to hurt her feelings.

"Of course," Carley smiled. "I hope you'll like it."

When Tillie opened the package, a beautiful rose colored bed comforter tumbled out and Tillie gasped. "It's gorgeous. Oh, Miss Carley you sure do know how to pick out lovely bed stuff."

"Thank you, Tillie. Now help me spread it out and then we'll be done here for the day."

They went back into the kitchen. Carley peeled and cut the vegetables, put them into the stew pot with the meat, added a cup of water, and then put the lid back on.

Carley walked into the ballroom to retrieve her pillow and sheets that she had been using for the past week.

"Hello, Miss Carley," Bucky chirped from a chair by the table, now covered with books and papers.

"Well, hello. What have we here?"

"I'm figuring out my schedule for school. I have to apply for classes this week and buy books I'll need."

"Have you noticed that used book store up on Pennsylvania Avenue? It's almost up to Washington Circle."

"Yes, I have. I got these two books there."

Carley picked one up and whistled. *"Gray's Anatomy,"* she read the title. "I thought you were going in for pharmacy. Isn't this a bit steep for the first year?"

"I'll tell you a little secret. Mother thinks I'm going to be a pharmacist, but I'm aiming to become a doctor. You see, she and Dad owned a Pharmacy in Morgantown. Dad died and Mother had to hire a pharmacist to take his place. She handles the rest of the store, you know, mustard plasters and such, and I ran the soda fountain."

"You were a soda jerk?" Carley grinned.

"Yes, Ma'am. And if I do say so myself, a pretty good one. At least all the girls from high school thought so. Why, Madam, if you want a majestic banana split, I'll put a split banana in the glass boat first. Then a scoop each of vanilla, chocolate with butterscotch, the strawberry with strawberry, and then whipped cream over all with a cherry on top."

"Whoa," Carley laughed, "I just gained ten pounds!"

"Mother says I bankrupted them trying to impress the girls," Bucky laughed.

"I can imagine. When do you intend telling your mother you're going to be a doctor?"

"She'll probably catch on when I send her my grades mid-term. As long as they're good, she'll be okay."

"Well, if you need to burn the midnight oil, you can do it here at this table. There's not a lot of space in your room. I know . . . it used to be mine."

"Thank you, Miss Carley. I'll have to be doing a lot of studying. Guess I'll have to give up going down to the

Gayety each weekend. For one thing, I won't be able to afford it."

"I tell you what, Bucky. If you want to entertain a young lady here. . . you know, play the rolls on the player piano or have a card game or checkers, you're welcome to bring her here, as long as you take her home by eleven."

"I'll think about that. It sure would be nice."

"All work and no play makes Bucky a dull boy, doesn't it?" A voice from the shady side of the room startled both Carley and Bucky.

"I didn't see you there, Mr. Foucher!" Bucky almost jumped out of his seat.

"Oh, I'm used to being overlooked. I'm the last of eleven children and the smallest. I could always get away with mischief, because I could hide easy."

"I bet you could," Bucky laughed.

"What kind of doctor do you intend to be? Besides a good one, of course." Wilbur asked.

"A family doctor. We don't have a lot of use for what they call 'specialists' in our town. If someone needs one real bad, they go to Pittsburgh."

"Can you get all you need to be a doctor at George-town?" Carley asked.

"I intend going on to Johns Hopkins to get my degree."

"Very ambitious," Wilbur said, standing up and taking his leave with a small bow to the two of them.

"I'll leave you alone with your books and applications," Carley said, going over to the chest of drawers standing under the window that looked out over the cellar doors. She lifted the top and took out the sheets and a pillow she had been using on the Chesterfield. Tucking them under her arm, she reached for the glass doorknob and turned to Bucky. "Can I get you a glass of iced tea, or perhaps lemonade?"

"Iced tea would be nice, but I'll come and get it. I could use a leg stretch."

Bucky followed Carley into the kitchen where she placed the sheets on top of the washing machine, and plopped the pillow in the rocking chair.

"Is Peter finished in your bedroom?" Bucky asked as he seated himself at the kitchen table.

"Yes, and he did an excellent job. In fact, much more than I imagined when we started the redecoration. The man has a real talent."

"None of my business, but why doesn't he do that instead of driving a bus all day and night?"

"He gets more driving. Not too many people are spending money fixing up in these bad money days. He says his father is just barely getting by."

"I guess you're right. I'm lucky my folks are in a necessary business in Morgantown. I know a couple of shops closed because they didn't get enough business."

Carley placed a tall glass of iced tea in front of Bucky and sat down across the table from him with a glass of her own.

Frances and Tillie came into the room with a mop and bucket. They had been cleaning the bathrooms. They quietly put the cleaning gear in the broom closet and picked up their burlap bags from under the stove.

"We'll see you in the morning. Have a good evening." Frances said, stepping out the screen door into the darkening back yard.

"They're such nice people," Bucky said, finishing up his glass of tea.

"Salt of the earth," Carley agreed. "Salt of the earth."

Nineteen

"That was a delicious breakfast, Miss Carley," Bill remarked. "I haven't had French toast for a long time."

"I thought you would all like a little change this morning. It looks like it is going to be a really gorgeous day."

"Hey, Eulali," Bucky said, "Bill and I went to your show. How about you coming to church with us this morning?"

Eulali looked down at her arms laden with bracelets and rings on each finger.

"I can't go looking like this."

"Sure you can. Our church doesn't tell anyone how to dress."

"If you've never been on stage at the Gayety, no one will recognize you, and if some men do and they're with their wives, they'll never let on they know you," Horace grinned.

"I'll go," Eulali said, standing up after gulping down her last piece of toast, "if I have a little time to make a couple of changes."

"No hurry. It's only quarter after nine and church doesn't start until eleven."

Eulali swept out of the room as Carley arose and began

gathering dishes to take to the kitchen. Frances and Tillie had been excused as usual, after serving the food, to go to their church.

Horace left to go visit his brother-in-law for the day. Peter was already driving his bus around the Lincoln Memorial.

Eulali came back into the dining room, minus all but one ring on each hand and wearing a white blouse that hung loosely from her shoulders. A long string of pearls graced her neck, and she certainly looked like a lady on her way to church.

Bucky smiled and gasped, "Is that you?"

Eulali laughed. "Didn't think I could dress like the respectable lady I am, did you?"

"Somehow I always thought all those beads were a costume to make you fit in down there at the Gayety," Carley smiled.

"Thank you," Eulali said.

Bill got up and Buddy immediately stood looking up at his master, as Bill gave him a small piece of bacon and patted his head. The dog wagged his tail in appreciation and the four, Bucky, Eulali, Bill and Buddy, like a small parade went through the hall to the door, out and down the concrete steps.

Carley stood watching them listen to the church bells singing out their chimes of invitation. She had never been much of a churchgoer. When she was little, before her mother had died, she had gone a few times to Sunday school with a little girl, Jessica, who lived in the apartments a block away. She was a schoolmate at Grant School just a few blocks up G Street.

Aunt Florence was proud to call herself an atheist. "I don't believe anyone ever came back from the dead," she said emphatically. "Once you're dead, you're dead. I believe in me, myself and I."

She didn't believe in friends, either, Carley thought to herself. Carley remembered Aunt Florence telling her all friends wanted was something from you. "Somehow, I just don't believe that," Carley said aloud as she turned back into the house and finished clearing the table.

⌒

The chickens had been cut for frying, the kale washed and put in the pot to cook, and the rice simmered on the stove. Sunday dinner would be served around four o'clock. She felt terribly lonely sitting in the shade of the maple tree in the backyard. Terry had been gone for three days and wouldn't be back for another six. He called each evening, but she really missed his presence when he would drop by at least once a day. Somehow, even the squirrels seemed to have deserted the yard.

Roger Clanahan, Terry's father, had suffered a heart attack and was in the hospital. Terry had obtained emergency leave for a week to take care of his mother and the homestead. Terry's brother, Daniel, would be coming to take over so Terry could come back to D. C.

Daniel was a "singing waiter" in New York City. He had a beautiful tenor voice and had headed to Broadway after he graduated from high school. However, Broadway didn't open up its arms to him. It seems, while Daniel could sing, he couldn't act. However, he made a good living as a singing waiter in a high-class restaurant, getting excellent tips from wealthy customers who appreciated his lovely Irish tenor.

Daniel was packing his clothes and vacating the room he had been renting for several years. He planned on staying in Edinburg, Virginia, as long as he was needed, even if it meant forever. He had been assured by his boss that he was welcome back at his old stand any time he wanted it.

Carley heard the chimes of the bank clock declare four o'clock, so she quickly hurried into the kitchen to start dinner. Frances and Tillie had returned and were busy setting the table for the Sunday meal.

"As soon as dinner is over, I'm going to go over to Lafayette Park and feed the squirrels," Carley said.

"You're going to do what?" Tillie asked.

"Feed the squirrels and pigeons. Haven't you ever done that as a child?"

"Oh, no," Frances said softly. "Even if we'd had money for peanuts, we black folks ain't welcome to loiter there."

Carley took a deep breath as she realized Frances was right.

"I hope one day that will change. I'm not proud of the way things are."

"Not your fault, Miss Carley. You treat us real good. Not like Mrs. Mertins did."

"Thank you, Frances. I really appreciate that."

The walk down G Street was pleasant, since a light shower had washed the dust from the day into the gutters and brightened the whole atmosphere of the city. She strolled slowly past the big executive office building and stopped at the corner where Gus stood by his peanut roasting cart, just in front of the White House. She purchased a small bag of peanuts and crossed Pennsylvania Avenue to enter Lafayette Square Park. The park was pretty crowded, but nonetheless, Carley found a green slatted bench beside the sidewalk crisscrossing a bright green grass carpet.

Looking around, Carley smiled at the huge grey statue of Frederick William Augustus Henry Ferdinand Baron Von Steuben astride his horse that stood in one corner. She had always wondered why anyone could name their little baby all those names. They probably called him 'Freddie,' she mused. She had hardly gotten seated when several pigeons and squirrels gathered around to be fed peanuts. Two squirrels jumped up onto the dark wood bench beside her and sat begging, their noses twitching in anticipation.

Carley remembered her mother bringing her here when she was little. The pigeons would fly up and sit on her head and, more times than not, when they go home shampooing would be needed. She hadn't been here since her mother had died. She had walked by on her way down to the stores, but she had never stopped to enjoy the sights and rest. It all came swarming back to mind, and she let out a deep sigh. Just then a big red dodge ball plopped into her lap spilling the peanuts onto the seat and through the slats. Carley looked up to see a little boy of about ten years standing in front of her. Before she could say anything, a little girl skipped up and stood behind him, her head hanging low, peeping around his arm. Her big brown eyes looked up through long blond lashes. Both children were generously endowed with freckles across their cheeks and noses.

A deep male voice made Carley look up to see a man, obviously their father, for he, too, had blond hair, brown eyes, and a face generously sprinkled with freckles.

"Tell the lady you're sorry you spilled her peanuts, and ask her nicely if you can please have your ball back?" he said.

"Can we have our ball back?" the boy asked.

"And what else?" the man urged his son.

"And I'm sorry I dumped your bag of peanuts," he mumbled, reaching out for the red toy that Carley held in her hands.

"That's quite all right, young man," Carley said holding out the ball. "The pigeons and squirrels were going to get them all anyway.

The children took the ball and were soon back on the grassy plot tossing it in the air and catching it. The father mumbled "Thank you" and left, crossing over to join a lady sitting on a bench holding a little baby.

Carley looked over her shoulder and saw two more benches housing what seemed to be families out having a loving time in the park on a beautiful Sunday afternoon.

Turning straight in her seat, Carley became deep in thought. Family love seemed to float on the air. There's a lot more to life than three meals a day and cleaning rooms, she thought.

She found herself unclasping the silver chain from around her neck and slipping the diamond ring into the palm of her hand. Folding her fingers around it, she fell into deep thought about what putting the ring on her finger

would mean. Love . . . of that she was certain . . . a family
. . . maybe . . . security . . . probably . . . a helpmate in all
her little daily problems . . . she hoped. As Carley realized
that the sun was beginning to slink down behind the buildings, she smiled, put the ring on her fourth finger of her
left hand, and stood. Shaking peanut debris from skirt and
picking up her small purse, she began the short walk back
to the manor.

A broad smile greeted anyone who happened to catch
her eye as she swung her arms and almost skipped up the
avenue.

As she entered the front hall she heard music emanating
from upstairs. Al Jolson singing "Mammy" blared forth and
as she looked up she saw Wilbur standing on the third-floor
landing, his door wide open. Next, she could hardly believe
her eyes, she saw Bill and Buddy come out of the door.

"Hello, Miss Carley," Wilbur said. "Do you like the music? I traded one of my still life paintings for a Victrola and
some records. The lady said she really wanted the painting,
but didn't have the money and seldom used the player."

"It sounds really good, Wilbur," Carley agreed, not taking her eyes off Bill, who was carefully coming down the
winding stairs holding onto both Buddy's harness handle
and the stair railing.

So, she thought, he could have been up on the third floor
the morning Aunt Florence fell.

Twenty

"Miss Carley," Frances announced, coming into the kitchen where Carley was flipping a new batch of pancakes from the skillet to the serving platter, "there's a man in the hallway who says he's your family."

"Family?" Carley asked, as she placed the platter in front of Bucky at the breakfast table on her way through the dining room. As she neared the tall, hefty man, she was swept up in his arms and swung around in a bear hug embrace.

"Carley, me lovely sister-in-law to be, hello, hello!" He set her on her feet in front of Frances, whose eyes were so big Carley thought they might pop out of her head.

"Daniel?" Carley laughed. "What are you doing here?"

Before Daniel could answer, Carley turned to Frances. "This is Terry's brother, Daniel, Frances. I've never met him but from Terry's description, I'd know him anywhere."

"Glad to meet you, Frances," Daniel said, extending his hand. Frances smiled broadly, shook his hand, then left to attend to the boarders in the dining room.

"How did you get here?" Carley asked.

"Took the train down from New York. My connection

with the Greyhound isn't until this afternoon. Planned it that way, so I could stop by and get acquainted."

"Have you had breakfast yet?"

"No. I kind of planned that, too. Terry has told me all about what a wonderful cook you are." He grinned.

As they entered the dining room, Daniel broke out into song, singing "My Wild Irish Rose" in his high tenor voice. Everyone looked up from their plates in astonishment.

"Sorry folks," Daniel explained, "A force of habit. When I see people eating at a table, I just gotta sing."

"Daniel is a singing waiter in a restaurant in New York City," Carley explained. "He's Terry's brother."

"I don't care whose brother he is," Eulali quipped. "He sure has a beautiful voice. He can sing at any meal I'm eating anytime."

"Thank you, lovely lady," Daniel bowed to her.

"Sit here," Carley said, pulling a chair from the wall beside the highboy and placing it next to her chair at the table. Before she could ask Frances to get another place setting, she same from the kitchen with a plate, napkin, and silver set. Tillie followed with a cup of steaming coffee.

"Help yourself to the pancakes, and I'll get your juice and sausages," Carley started to go to the kitchen when Tillie passed her and told her to go sit down, that she would take care of it.

Carley made introductions all around as conversation turned into a quiz session.

"Let the man eat," Carley smiled at the group.

"I don't mind," Daniel said between bites. "I have questions of my own. Terry has told me so much about you. And before you ask, it's all good. It's as if I already know you."

"Tell me about New York," Eulali asked. "I worked there once. I was a high kicker in a chorus line."

"You were a what?" Carley gasped.

"A high kicker. It's a dance routine where you put your arms around the shoulders of the girls next to you and kick one leg, then the other, as high as you can without falling over backwards," Eulali laughed.

"How long did you do that?" Bucky asked giving all his attention to his flashy friend.

"Until I got typhoid in an epidemic. It took me a couple of months to get better. I never regained enough strength for the rigid routines, so I had to quit. I didn't have talent for anything else on stage, so I began working in the wardrobe back stage."

"How did you end up here in D.C.?" Daniel asked. "It's a long way from Broadway."

"A group of specialty dancers got a contract with the Gayety here and convinced me that the winters were warmer. They needed me to look after their costumes . . . so I came south."

"How about you, Daniel? How'd you get from Edinburg to the big city?"

"Well, everyone kept telling me I had a voice that I should use beyond singing in the choir. So as soon as I graduated from High School, I took off for the city to let the Great White Way know what a treasure they had in a country boy. Oh, they thought I had a great voice, but it wasn't long before they found out I can't act worth a darn. So, I ended up as a singing waiter to earn my corned beef and cabbage."

He sounded so happy about his situation, it was hard to feel badly that he failed at his dream of working on Broadway.

"What are your plans now?" Eulali asked.

"Well, as you probably know, I'm needed back home. Terry has a good job here, and he really doesn't care for truck farming. I liked it myself . . . if I remember correctly. So, I think everything is going to work out fine.

⌒

"Let's go out and sit on the bench under the maple. I'll bring a tray of lemonade and chips," Carley suggested to Daniel. "You have a few hours yet before you have to catch your bus. I wish you could stay longer."

"Lemonade sounds wonderful. You know, Carley, you're everything Terry has told me about you."

"Oh, what did he say?"

"Lovely. Good cook. Gracious. Oh, I could go on. He's lucky to have you as a wife."

"Has he told you I've never said 'yes' yet?"

"Oh yeah. But he said he didn't believe you. My brother has a big ego. He can't think anyone would turn him down, once he became determined to woo and win," Daniel smiled at Carley.

"Well, just so you know . . . I have decided to take him

up on his proposal. But don't tell him I said so. You see, I wouldn't wear the ring until I was sure."

"I see you have the ring on." Daniel observed.

"Yes, I just put it on when I realized how much I was missing him. He calls often, but I miss seeing him every day when he stops in for a cup of coffee."

"I won't tell him, although, I'm sure he'll ask."

"What about you? You've never been married? I'm certain you've had your bevy of girls hanging around such a handsome Irish singer."

"Like Terry, I'm very particular. Yes, I've had a lot of girl-friends, but so far, none I'd want to spend the rest of my life with."

"Maybe when you get back home you'll find someone who likes to cook and keep house instead of partying all the time."

"Could be . . . could be." Daniel smiled. Carley's heart gave a jump; his smile was just like his brothers. She found herself being anxious to see Terry again, but she knew she would have to wait another four days for him to find out how much she loved him.

Bidding Daniel goodbye at the front door, Carley turned to hear Peter give a whoop from the second floor.

"I knew it! I knew it" he shouted.

"Knew what?" Carley asked climbing the stairs.

"Look here, Miss Carley. There's a hidden drawer in back of the fireplace." Peter pointed to a small drawer pulled out from behind the chimney in back of the black marble mantle. In his hands he held a variety of candles.

Carley smiled. "I bet they were spares for the candlesticks that used to be up here. If I remember correctly, Aunt Florence had the candlesticks put away because she didn't want to take a chance on someone stealing them. She wasn't about to pay for new ones. Maybe I can locate the holders somewhere and restore the mantle's decorations."

"They look funny. Not like any candles I ever saw."

"They're handmade—probably in the kitchen. There has to be a candle mold around somewhere. Maybe I can find that too."

"One of these days, Miss Carley, I would like to investigate the attic. I can just imagine the treasures I might find there."

"I'll have to think a bit on that, Peter. It's actually been my intention to do just as you suggest one of these winter days when the attic isn't too hot. I'm sure there's a lot of history up there, but I'm also certain there's a lot of trash that has never been thrown away."

Peter smiled as he returned the candles to their secret drawer and carefully pushed it back in place.

Carley went into the kitchen to begin stirring up biscuit dough and searing chipped beef to make gravy for dinner. Baked apples with cinnamon and vanilla ice cream would round out the meal.

"Frances, did you hear what Peter found in the den?"

"No, ma'am. I heard you two talking, but it's not my place to eavesdrop." Frances said, acting as though she never tried to overhear talk whenever she could. Carley knew better, but she would never accuse her of deliberately snooping. She is just curious, not gossipy.

Carley told her about the candles and Frances told her the candle mold was up in a drawer in the musty maid's room over the kitchen.

"Do you know how to make them? I mean, what makes the wax?"

"No, I don't. But there is an old lady that lives near Georgetown Circle that knows, I'm pretty sure."

"Well, there's no hurry to find out. Just when you think about it, maybe around the holiday we can make some special candles to burn on our mantles. Make it kind of festive."

"When does Mr. Terry get home?" Tillie asked.

"Some time Sunday. I'm planning a special dinner. Lemon meringue pie for dessert. That's his favorite."

"Miss Carley, I just noticed that ring on your finger. Does that mean what I think it does?" Frances grinned.

"Yes, but don't go congratulating him yet. I haven't said 'yes' to him yet. He gave me the ring in July, but I told him I wouldn't wear it until I was really sure. I'm sure now."

"Oh, I'll not breathe a word until you say I can." Both ladies looked conspiratorially at each other.

Carley pulled the sheet up to her neck after she had turned the light off beside her bed. Looking around the room, she was still amazed at the wonderful transition Peter had wrought. He really seemed to be a very sweet fellow, but still, she thought, he had what seemed to be an uncontrollable temper. Putting thoughts of Peter out of her mind, she began to dream of Terry and his return. She would splurge and have pounded steak, baked potatoes and green beans with mushrooms for his welcome home dinner. They would make the announcement, but she wasn't quite ready to set a date. There was too much to do and a murder to solve first.

Twenty-one

F luffy white clouds skittered across a clear early autumn sky as Carley watched a flock of Canadian geese wing their way home. The brisk breeze shook down some acorns from the oak in the further corner of the yard, and several fat furry squirrels scampered to snatch them up and bury them in the soft soil beneath the roses in the garden.

Jolie will have a busy time digging them up before they have a chance to sprout. He'll get them out of there, Carley thought. He didn't like tiny trees growing around the flowers.

It seemed a perfect day. It was Friday, and Terry was due home some time Sunday.

"Miss Carley," Tillie's voice called. "The mailman is here, and he has a package for Mr. Owens. Says it needs to be signed for, but he isn't in his room. I knocked, and the door came open a bit, but he didn't answer. Mailman says you sign for it."

"I'm coming, Tillie," Carley walked quickly through the back door to the hall.

"I'll sign," she took the brown paper wrapped package and signed the slip the mailman held out to her on a clipboard.

"Thank you ma'am," he smiled. "Just have to let the sender know a responsible adult got it."

"I understand," Carley took the rest of the mail out of his hand and turned to sort it on the table. She watched the mailman go slowly down the stairs, reaching into his leather shoulder bag for mail to deliver further down the street.

Carley decided to take Horace's mail up to his room and climbed the winding stairs to the second floor hall. Passing by Eulali's door, she smiled to herself as she heard Eulali plopping several bars of soap into her bathtub.

Eulali's room was the largest in the house, which had originally been built by Carley's great-great grandparents. It had a tub and a sink, one of the first ever in a house, she had been told. The room had a marble mantled fireplace, and Carley remembered a huge canopied bed against the side wall. A six-drawered dresser and two chests had sat against the wall, and the room still had not seemed filled.

She knocked on Horace's door and felt it open wider. She stepped inside and saw the top of his dresser filled with papers. Deciding to leave the package and the rest of the mail on top of the pile, she stepped across the room and put them down.

Her eyes went wide when she accidently glimpsed two insurance policies stamped "Paid in full". One was a policy for Beatrice, and the other was for her grandmother, Florence Mertins. Picking it up, she read the line stating who would get the payout. H. William Owens was the beneficiary! It took Carley only a second to realize the "H" was Horace. He had gained two thousand dollars at her grandmother's death.

The policy for Beatrice was for fifteen thousand dollars.

"What are you snooping around for?" Horace's voice was just behind her, and she jumped. He had been so quiet entering the room that she had failed to realize he was there.

"I'm not snooping. I just had a package for you that needed to be signed for, and I thought I would bring it up. But since you mentioned it, how come you had a life insurance policy in my grandmother's name and with you as the beneficiary? I need an explanation, and it better be a good one."

"Yes, I can explain." Horace reached for the policy in Carley's hand.

"I bet you can. I'm quite certain Aunt Florence never gave you permission."

"Well, you're right, and perhaps my explanation may not be satisfactory to you, but," he said hesitantly, taking a deep breath, "my company was having a competition with a pretty good bonus to the most productive salesman, and I only needed one more policy to win. I just used her name; I paid the monthly premium, which was very little."

"I doubt you turned the premium in, did you?" Not waiting for an answer, she continued. "And you probably had to fake a health certificate, too." She remembered the physical she had gone through for her own policy Aunt Florence insisted she needed.

"Well, yes. But a lot of salesmen do that. We have a doctor who gets a few dollars behind his back. There's really no harm done. Times are rough all over."

"Comforting to know you work for an honest company,

but rather to the point, you had two thousand reasons to want Aunt Florence dead, didn't you?"

Carley was surprised at herself. She had always shied away from confrontations, and here she was accusing Horace of the act of murder.

"Oh, no Miss Carley," Horace's face turned a brilliant red. "I would never do anything like that. Besides I wasn't here. I had already gone to work."

"Nevertheless, you aren't the honest man I thought you were, or one I want here in my house. I want you to leave. Today, if that is possible." Carley surprised herself with the anger in her voice.

"I was leaving, anyway." Horace almost snapped at her. "I was going to give you my two weeks' notice, but now that won't be necessary. Janet eloped with her young doctor suitor last week, and George wants me to move in and take her room."

"Good. At least I won't have to feel guilty for throwing you out on the street."

Carley was almost trembling in rage. Looking straight in his eyes she held out her hand.

"I'll have the keys to your room and the front door."

Horace walked over to his coat hanging on the bedpost and retrieved the keys from his pocket and handed them to her.

"Oh, yes, another thing," Carley nearly spat out. "You better go to the Post Office and put in your change of address. Any mail coming here will be marked return to sender from now on."

Horace's face reflected astonishment, but he said nothing more.

She turned on her heels and marched out of the room, her shoulders stiff and aching. She could not recall when she had been so angry.

"Miss Carley," Frances came up to her in the hallway. "Are you all right? You look madder than a wet hen."

"I'll be fine as soon as I sit down with a cup of tea, Frances. Then, I'll tell you all about it."

Frances hurried to the kitchen and put on the kettle, as Carley stepped out the back door to get another look at the autumn scene. "How could such a perfect day get so messed up so quickly?" She thought out loud.

Going back in and sitting down at the table, she waited for the kettle to whistle and Frances to pour the boiling water over the tea leaves in the china teapot. It would only take a couple of minutes to steep.

"Mr. Owens is leaving today, Frances. I have discovered he is far from an honest man."

"Our Mr. Owens?" Frances put her hand over her mouth.

Carley told her the bare details.

"Suffice to say. I have proof of it, or at least, I have seen proof." Carley regretted she hadn't demanded her grandmother's policy, but then, she doubted he would have given it to her. She would tell Terry about it at the first opportunity.

Carley was sitting in the ballroom trying to concentrate on the newspaper when she looked up through the glass

French doors to the hallway and saw Horace thumb through the telephone book and then use the phone. He then went up the stairs and soon returned with two large cloth valises and a smaller leather suitcase. He stood by the door until Carley heard the sound of a horn beeping. She went over to the window and looked out to see a Yellow Cab parked at the curb and the cabbie helping Horace put his bags in the back. Horace took a long look at the house and for a moment saw Carley in the window. He then climbed in the cab, allowing the whole disagreeable afternoon to sweep away. She breathed a deep sigh of relief and went into the kitchen determined to put her efforts toward dinner.

Bucky, Bill, Wilbur and Peter were at the table. Eulali was at work.

"I need to tell you all something, folks. Horace has left us. He has moved in with his brother-in-law, George. It seems his niece, Janet, the nurse, eloped last week with a young doctor and has moved out. George asked Mr. Owens to come live with him and so he has."

"Didn't give you much notice, did he?" Peter remarked.

"No, but that's all right," Carley said dismissing the subject.

Frances just smiled to herself like a satisfied cat. She knew the whole story, but she wouldn't tell.

Twenty-two

Saturday morning breakfast dishes had been cleared away, and Frances and Tillie had gone upstairs to take the soiled linens from Horace's bed for laundering. The room would need a thorough cleaning before renting again. The brass bed would need polishing and the windows would need washing on the inside.

"Miss Carley, come look!" Frances was hurrying through the dining room to the kitchen where Carley was sitting at the table planning Terry's welcome home dinner for the next day.

"What is it, Frances?"

"Mr. Owens left all Mrs. Owen's things laid out all over the place."

"What?" Carley rose from the table and hurried behind Frances through the hall and up the stairs.

Sure enough, when Carley looked into the room she saw clothes strewn everywhere. It looked like he had gone through every pocket, for they were all turned inside out, and all the drawers in the bureau were hanging open and mostly empty.

"I guess he didn't have anyone to give them to, but he

could have asked if we knew of any who would want them." Carley observed.

"Ms. Owens was a little woman. These are all much too small for us, even you, Miss Carley."

"You're right there, Frances. I'll tell you what. Call over to the grocery and see if they have about three or four clean cardboard cartons that we can have."

"Yes ma'am," Frances started toward the door.

"Oh yes," Carley stopped her, "there is a list on the kitchen table of things I need. Take money from the box and go get them, too. Don't try to carry them all. Get the delivery boy to bring them on his wagon. Give him a dime."

"All right. I'm on my way." Frances said as she went through the door.

Carley turned to the mess in the room. She started picking up each dress and coat on the bed, straightening it and gently placing it in a pile. Soon she had blouses, skirts, dresses, hats and coats in a great sorted heap on the bed. Shoes and slippers were neatly lined up on the floor in front of the window.

Most drawers were empty, but a couple held underwear and handkerchiefs.

"These hankies are beautiful," Tillie picked one up and showed it to Carley. It had tatting all around the edge with tiny embroidered roses in one corner.

Carley picked the pile of about two dozen hankies and looked at them.

"They all look handmade. Someone, I wonder if it was

Beatrice, lovingly made each one of these. They are lovely
—just beautiful."

"They sure are," Tillie agreed tenderly running her fingers over a yellow and green daisy.

"Tell you what," Carley said. "We are going to put all
the clothes in the cartons your mother is bringing back. I'll
put them in the attic for a few months, and if Mr. Owens
doesn't come back for them we'll give them to the needy.
But, I'm going to keep these little beauties in my nightstand,
and we'll divvy them up between the three of us when the
time comes. Small enough pay for all the trouble with these
clothes," she said with a smile, almost a smirk, on her face.

Tillie's face shone as she reluctantly handed the hanky
she was fondling back to Carley.

Looking at the mess Horace had left, Carley shook her
head. I really thought I knew Horace, but I guess I didn't,
Carley mused to herself. Remembering the tone of his voice
and the brazen pride of his deception to his employer, Carley was beginning to think him capable of almost anything
. . . perhaps even murder.

Tillie had washed a load of towels and the sheets and
pillowcases from Horace's room and had hung them out to
dry. Frances was busy shining the brass bed; a chore Carley
remembered was her job when she was a little girl. She
hated the smelly cream she had had to use. It stained her
fingers for weeks, it seemed. That, and doing the dishes,
had been her lot because they took time, and neither her
mother nor her Aunt Florence had wanted to take the time

to do them. She had always hated both chores, since she couldn't remember when, and was glad Tillie and Frances did them cheerfully.

Carley looked through her "Joy of Cooking" cookbook for a special cake for Terry's home coming tomorrow. His mother would have already filled him with apple and peach pies. Carley wanted to find something unusual.

"Ah hah," she cried aloud, "Boston cream pie".

"'Boston Cream', it's really cake and it's delicious."

"How you make that?"

"You take one layer of cake, cut it into two layers, put vanilla pudding between them and top it with melted chocolate icing."

"I had a piece at Tillie's wedding. Somebody had bought it at a bakery," Frances said, "I wondered what it was but didn't get a chance to find out."

"Did you finish upstairs?"

"Mostly, but the floor needs a coat of wax. Can I wait until Monday to do that?"

"Of course. There's no big hurry."

Peter knocked on the door jamb, and Carley looked up from her recipes.

"Can I talk to you for a minute?" Peter asked.

"Sure, sit down."

"Well, sometime in the near future I hope to be getting married."

"Congratulations," Carley smiled.

"Well, I haven't asked her yet, but I'm pretty sure she'll

say 'yes'. We've been seeing each other a couple of times a week for a long time and, well, I'm really in love with her. Her name's Roberta. Her folks are teachers and she is a file clerk at The Agriculture Department down on 14th Street."

"Sounds like they are a real nice family."

"What I would like to ask is if I could have the room Mr. Owens left. It's much bigger than mine. Be nicer for two."

That's fine with me, Peter. In fact, if you would like to do some redecorating before you move into it, you're welcome to. I'll buy the paint and paper."

Peter's face lit up with that news and as he stood up he put his arms around Frances and gave her a peck on the cheek.

Frances, obviously surprised, but pleased, put her hand to her cheek and smiled. "Thank you, Mr. Peter."

Peter looked down at Carley's hand and noticed the ring she was wearing. His face lit up and this smile stretched ear to ear.

"You and Terry?"

Carley followed where he was looking and grinned.

"Yes, but he doesn't know yet, so don't say anything if you see him before I do."

"What do you mean, he doesn't know?"

"Well, he asked me to marry him on July fourth at the fireworks display and put the ring on my finger. I took it off and gave it back, but he managed to give it back to me. I've worn it on a chain around my neck since, and told him when I am sure I'd put it back on."

"What made you sure?"

"He's been gone almost ten days, and I sure have missed him. I guess the adage 'absence makes the heart grow fonder' really is true. At least it has worked on me. Now promise, if you see Terry first when he comes tomorrow, you won't say anything . . . to anybody. I don't want someone saying 'congratulations' before I've talked to him."

"Mum's the word." Peter said, rising from his chair and heading back into the dining room.

⌐

After dinner had been cleared away and both Frances and Tillie had gone home, Carley went into the ballroom where Bill was entertaining on the grand piano playing a Strauss waltz. I must get the piano tuned, Carley thought. It sounded okay, but it had never been tuned as far as Carley could remember.

Bucky was curled up with a book, and Wilbur had the newspaper spread out in front of him on the table next to the Morris chair. Carley had brought in a cookbook and pad of paper to do her favorite thing, make menus for the following week.

Bill had finished the waltz and had begun Beethoven's 'Fir Elise', when the doorbell rang. Carley stepped into the hallway, shutting the door behind her. Opening the door, she was surprised to see Lawrence Wampler standing there with his suitcase. A Checkered Cab pulled away from the curb.

"Well, hello there," Carley greeted Bill's brother. He stepped through the door and stopped quickly.

"Is that Bill playing?" he whispered.

"Yes, isn't it beautiful?"

"I don't remember when I last heard him at the keyboard. Let's sneak in. I want to hear it all."

Silently as possible, Carley opened the doors and both stepped into the room. Carley noticed a smile come to Bill's lips, but he kept on playing. Soon as the last note wafted into the air, he turned and said, "Welcome, Brother Larry. I've been waiting for you."

Larry rushed up to him and gave him a big bear-hug before he could even rise from the bench.

"Well, look who's here," Wilbur said. "Glad to see you, Larry."

Bucky looked up from his book, closed it and stood extending his hand. "I'm Bucky Keller, Mr. Wampler."

"Billy has told me all about you, Bucky, and please, call me Larry."

"Have you had anything to eat?" Carley asked.

"I was going to take Bill out to the diner on the Avenue."

"He's already had dinner. If you would like a meatloaf sandwich, I'd be glad to make one for you."

"If it's no trouble, that sounds great," Larry agreed.

"No trouble at all. Let's go out to the kitchen. I think there was leftover pie, too."

They were soon settled at the table, and Larry was telling about his journey and making plans for his stay. "I can put a cot in the den for you, Larry. Right now, I don't have a clean vacant room," Carley explained.

"No, need," Bill said. "Larry and I have slept together since we were little babies. It would be a bit odd to sleep apart in the same house."

"Okay, whatever you want, just let me know, and you'll get it if I have it," Carley offered. I'll get you a fresh towel and washcloth."

⁓

Carley had just finished cleaning up the dishes and putting them away when Wilbur came into the room.

"Miss Carley," he said rather timidly, "Can I have a word with you?"

"Of course, Wilbur. What's up?"

"I thought I would tell you what I saw today when I was out peddling my pictures."

"And what was that?"

"I was going down the Avenue past the park when I saw Mr. Owens coming toward me. He had a lady on his arm looking up at him rather adoringly. He had a carnation in his lapel. He saw me and put his hand to the brim of hat, but he didn't stop to talk and just walked on with his head turned to her. Probably explaining how he knew such a crumby little guy in black."

"Don't put yourself down. You are a very good artist earning an honest living, which is more than I can say for at least one person."

"But it's hardly a month or so since he buried poor Beatrice, his wife!" Wilbur was indignant.

"I agree. And you would think he could have asked how we all were, wouldn't you?" Carley exclaimed.

Twenty-three

"CONGRATULATIONS" rang out from all around the dinner table as Terry came into the dining room. Terry looked mystified as he looked around and then caught Carley's grim face as she looked straight at Peter who shrugged his shoulders, and put both palms up to denote his innocence. Carley then looked at Frances and Tillie who stood slowly shaking their heads with a broad smile on their faces.

Carley then put her hand up to her mouth and Terry gave a whoop . . . he saw his ring on her finger. He rushed around the table and swept her up in a big hug.

"We'll talk later," Carley smiled.

Frances and Tillie began serving the dinner of pounded steak smothered with brown gravy and mashed potatoes and green beans with slivered almonds and mushrooms. An individual salad sat by each plate.

"It's my fault," Eulali said.

"What is?" Carley looked at her.

"I told everyone that you were engaged to Terry."

"How did you know? I didn't tell anyone."

"Well, on July fourth, Terry showed me the ring, asking if it was good enough for you. I guess he thought I was an expert on jewelry," Eulali held up her hand and shook her wrist, making them jangle. "I told him it was a lovely ring, but that you'd be happy with a paper cigar band."

"I would have at that," Carley laughed.

"When you weren't wearing the ring—when you came home—I asked Terry what had happened. He told me you had the ring, but you weren't really quite sure, but that you'd put it on as soon as you made up your mind. I noticed the other day you had it on . . . and then I told. I'm sorry if you are angry with me. I didn't mean to meddle."

Carley went around the table and gave the distraught Eulali a hug. That's okay, honey. We're all family here. Now let's eat this dinner before it gets cold. Make sure to save room for Boston Cream pie."

Terry looked across the table and nudged Carley. "Who's the new knight of our round table?"

Carley looked over and said softly, "That's Lawrence Wampler, Bill's brother. He's just here for this week."

Terry smiled at Larry when he caught his eye. "I understand you are the safety pin genius."

Larry laughed heartily, "So Billy's been telling tales out of school. Yes, we devised that little clothing system quite some time ago. It wasn't all my idea. We worked it out together."

"It was mostly Larry's idea," Bill quickly corrected him, "I sure didn't know when I was wearing brown, grey and black together."

"I'm Terry Clanahan," Terry introduced himself. "As you

have just learned, Carley and I are going to be married. We haven't worked out when yet, but we will, won't we?" He turned to Carley. She smiled at him and bit into her pie rather than answer.

"By the way," Larry said, "Billy and I are going to the Gayety next Friday, my last day here, and you are invited to come."

"I'll be on duty then, but maybe Bucky will join you."

"Not me," Bucky quickly declined. "I have a date for the movies. A really nice girl that I would never take to a burlesque. Not that you aren't a really nice lady, Miss Eulali, but you, well, you're different." Bucky blushed and Eulali quickly stepped in to ease his agony.

"That's all right, dear. I know what you are saying. Really nice girls don't go to hooch shows, and I agree with you. If I didn't work there, I wouldn't go either," she paused, "if you believe that, I'd like to sell you the Brooklyn Bridge."

"Not to change the subject, Terry, but how is your father?" Peter asked.

"He's still in the hospital, but he's doing fine. The doctor seems to think he'll be coming home in a couple of weeks. Of course, he'll have to take it easy for a few months. He was pretty ill. Almost died."

"I'm glad to hear he's getting better. Heart attacks are very serious business."

"Oh, Wilbur, I told Mom about you coming down to paint scenery. She said to come right along, but told me to warn you that she might put you to work."

"I wouldn't mind that," Wilbur smiled. "I used to slop pigs as a boy on my grandpop's farm."

"We'll plan on it in a couple of weeks, when I go down to help put the hay in the barn. Dan's still a bit rusty on farm work, but he's doing just fine."

Conversation soon murmured into sighs of satisfaction as pie plates were cleaned shiny, and one by one the diners left to go to other pursuits for Sunday afternoon.

"Miss Carley," Frances said, "Why don't you and Mr. Terry go on to yourselves. Tillie and I will clean everything up. Jolie will be here with Stanley, and I saved enough to feed them both, including that wonderful pie."

Carley looked gratefully at the ladies and, taking Terry by the arm, led him out into the garden to their favorite bench beneath the big maple tree. Before they could sit down, Terry turned Carley to face him and, putting his arms around her, he bent his head and kissed her hungrily. She put a palm of her hand on his cheek and returned the kiss passionately. As they drew apart, Terry held her left hand and looked at the ring.

"When did you decide to wear it?"

"A few days ago, when I was feeding squirrels in Lafayette Park."

"When you were doing what?" His eyebrows rose up on his forehead.

"I was lonesome. The house seemed empty and, of course, you weren't here—and Terry, I really did miss you so much."

"What has missing me to do with squirrels? Or maybe I don't want to know," he laughed.

"Well, as I was sitting there, a little boy and his sister were playing catch with a red ball. It ended up in my lap and the little boy came over with his sister to ask for it. Their father came over to tell them to apologize to me. He was so loving to them, and they were so behaved. I looked over my shoulder and saw their mother on a bench with another little child. They looked so happy. I realized then that was what I wanted. A happy family."

"Hadn't you seen happy families before?"

"No. Not really. You see, as you know, my mother died when I was ten. I know she loved me and I loved her, but after that it was Aunt Florence, and she never had any love for me or anyone. I wasn't allowed to have friends from school in, nor allowed to go to the playground or anyone else's house."

They sat in silence for a brief moment, then Carley smiled as she looked at her ring.

"Then I knew, for sure, you were the one I wanted to be my husband, and I took the ring off the chain and put it on my finger. It feels so good there—so right." She looked up at him adoringly.

Terry put his arm around her shoulder, and they both looked a bit startled as orchestra music floated in the air from the roof garden of the hotel. The sun had lowered in the sky, making fuzzy the sharp shadows previously outlining the trees. They sat content, ignoring the evening chill for quite some time, both absorbed in their own thoughts.

Finally, Terry broke the silence. "What's been going on since I left?"

Carley straightened her back, and took a deep breath.

"I think I know who killed Aunt Florence."

"You do? Who?" Terry turned to face her.

"Well, I guess you didn't notice Horace Owens was not at the table. He's gone. I kicked him out."

"You did what? Why?" Terry sounded shocked and very mystified.

"Well, to make a long story short, I found out he had a two-thousand-dollar life insurance policy on Aunt Florence."

"He did? Did you get the money?"

"No. HE was beneficiary. He had paid the premiums— or so he said he did."

"But she must have had a doctor examine her for him to get the policy."

"He paid a crooked doctor to okay the policy. He told me so. Said a lot of salesmen do it."

"But why?"

"Some competition among salesmen to get a bonus for the most policies, or something."

Terry rubbed his chin with his fingers, his mind trying to absorb what she was telling him.

"Where did he go?"

"He's living with George, his brother-in-law. When I told him to leave, he said he was going to leave in a couple of weeks anyway. He left the day we had our confrontation. Left a mess behind. All of Beatrice's clothes thrown all over the room, the pockets turned inside out. I guess he searched them for extra change she might have left in them."

"What are you going to do with them?"

"I had Frances and Tillie box them up and put them in the attic. If he hasn't come for them in a couple of months, I'll donate them to the mission shelter for Christmas."

"Good thinking. You know, though, we don't have any proof he pushed your grandmother over the railing."

"I know. But another thing happened. Bill Wampler is on my list. I found he can climb those stairs to the third floor and could have been up there."

"How do you know?" Terry asked.

"I heard music coming from Wilbur's open door, and when I looked up, I saw Bill leave the room and come back down the steps. He's very adept at navigating stairs, even circular ones."

"Who else is on your list?"

"Eulali. If Aunt Florence had found out she worked where she does, she would most certainly have told her to leave."

"That leaves Peter. Is he on the list, too?"

"Well," Carley hesitated, "He does have a temper he can't control. Aunt Florence could have easily provoked him to rage. I felt like doing her bodily harm a couple of times myself. But I would just walk away," Carley smiled.

Terry squeezed her shoulder, and they both looked up

202 Room, Board *and* Murder

into the dark sky to see the big Goodyear blimp floating by with a lit-up tail of advertisement.

"The city sky certainly is different from down in the country. When it gets dark down there all we see is the moon and stars, and instead of dance music from a hotel, we hear frogs and crickets."

Twenty-four

The morning's peace was shattered by the sound of hammering as Carley looked out the window to see Peter replacing the cellar door. He had found planks somewhere to not only fix the broken door but also to replace it entirely. She raised the window and shouted down to him.

"Where did you get all that wood?"

Peter looked up and smiled. "The last time I went over to Dad's place, I found a stash he had put aside because they weren't good for making cabinets. He gave them to me, wouldn't let me pay anything for them. He does things like that all the time. That's why Mom has to sew other people's clothes."

Carley sighed as she realized how bitter Peter was about his mother having to sew for other people.

"The next time you are going home let me know, and I'll bake a cake", Carley laughed.

"It's a deal." Peter bent over his work, and Carley shut the window and went back to her cookbook.

"This is corned beef and cabbage weather," she mused. "And raisin pie," she said aloud as she shut the book and returned it to the shelf.

Looking out the screen door, she saw Jolie pruning back the roses. He had been working hard to get the bushes ready for winter—raking up bushels of leaves and setting them aside near the back fence for compost. He was a very good gardener. Carley smiled to herself. I'm so lucky to have him, she thought to herself. So far, her first few months at being head of a boarding house had been successful, thanks to so many nice people. They had, she decided, really become family.

"Mr. Owen's room is ready for rent," Frances announced. "Everything has been waxed, polished and shined." She put the jar of brass polish back on the shelf under the sink and tossed the rags into the empty washer.

"Peter is moving in. His room will be the vacant one."

"How come?" Frances seemed surprised.

"Because he's in love," Carley smiled. "He has a girl-friend. He thinks maybe when he asks her to marry him, she'll say yes. Don't say I told you . . . just wait."

Before they could say anything more, they heard Peter scream and cuss badly. When they looked out the door, they saw Jolie with a smoking newspaper in his hand. It seemed he had found a bumblebee's nest in a hole in the old wood fence that circled the yard. He was smoking them out when one of them zoned in on poor Peter bent over the cellar door. It had stung him in the rear through flimsy thin summer cotton painter's pants.

Both ladies put their hands over their ears. "Now not a word to anyone," Carley reminded Frances.

"Not a word, but I hope she's aware of that temper, Miss Carley. I'm not sure he's good marriage material."

"Perhaps she can tame him," Carley laughed at Frances' remark. "And I think he's going to paint the Owenses' room—or should I say his room—a different color."

Carley picked up her change purse and a small marketing basket.

"I'll be back soon; I just want to get a good corned beef brisket from Nick and Johnny's. Watch those raisins, please, I don't want them to cook long."

⌒

As she turned the corner onto G Street, she heard Nick's beautiful voice wafting on the breeze. He always practiced his operatic arias with an open window in the summertime. Often he would draw an audience under the trees in front of the deli he and his brother, Johnny, ran. Today, she was amused to see a small brown and white terrier sitting in the tree box, his mouth drawn into a small "O" singing along with Nick. Nick was a big Greek with black curly hair and a bushy mustache above a large smile. He was always in good humor, and the neighborhood kids loved him. He belonged to the local amateur opera group that entertained at several auditoriums around the city.

Carley stepped through the door to a blend of wonderful aromas, including dill pickles in one barrel and pig's feet, also pickled, in another. A couple of flies came in the door as she entered, but they were soon doomed to the sticky fly paper strings hanging from the ceiling.

"Afternoon, Miss Mertins," Johnny greeted her. "What can I do for you today?"

"I need a brisket of corned beef."

Johnny immediately turned to the large refrigerator. He brought out the meat and placed it on a piece of waxed paper torn from the roll that hung over the back counter which held wood racks slotted for knives of every size. He presented the meat for Carley's approval, and when she smiled and nodded her head, he wrapped it tightly with cord pulled from a large cone of white string.

Carley looked around, and her eyes fell upon jars of olives on the shelves. She reached for a pint jar filled with dark brown Greek olives. She loved them and had often bought them for herself. She had once offered one to Frances and Tillie, but they had taken one bite of the aged olive, had made screwed-up faces and had spit them out. Carley never tried to serve them to the boarders, for they were too expensive. She didn't feel a bit guilty keeping them to herself. Her boarders were always well fed—at least she had few leftovers.

Carley purchased a jar of powdered garlic to mix with butter and spread on French bread slices to go with the evening's meal.

Stepping out the door into the afternoon sunshine, her purchases tucked away in the basket hanging from her arm, Carley saw several people laughing at the little dog, so seriously accompanying Nick's song. Her mind went back to when she was a little girl, and her great grandfather and grandmother had friends in to enjoy an evening filled with music around the grand piano. It had been so long ago, and when they died the music stopped. Maybe, she thought, I'll start it up again. But then, she realized, she didn't have a circle of friends like her great grandparents had enjoyed. Aunt Florence had never had friends, none that Carley knew of. She certainly hadn't been cordial to anyone.

Walking back to the manor, Carley thought hard about who, other than her boarders, she would invite. She realized she didn't have any close friends from school—Aunt Florence wouldn't allow her to bring anyone home. She had to come directly home to take care of her duties of dusting and ironing. The same routine went on even after she had graduated and had begun working at the Florist.

"Oh, well," she said aloud to nobody else. "No sense brooding over what was. I have a good life. I have Terry," she smiled at the thought as she entered the kitchen door.

"You look like somebody told you that you won a million dollars," Tillie smiled.

"Just happy, I guess. Just saw that little dog singing along with Nick. He's so cute."

"Maybe you ought to get a pooch," Frances quipped.

"Buddy being here is quite enough," Carley smiled. "I have enough to do."

"Yes'm," Tillie agreed. "Stan brought home a little kitten the other day. She's cute as a button. We're training her to use a newspaper, and once she gets a little bigger, I guess we'll have to take her out to the backyard a couple times a day."

"What color is she?"

"Just a regular old tabby."

"Bring her one day; I'd like to see her. Bring her Sunday afternoon. We can keep her in the kitchen."

"I wonder what Buddy will think about her. I bet he'll like her." Tillie smiled. "She's still in a box with high sides in the apartment."

"How big a box?"

"One that's pretty tall. We had a table we bought at the store delivered in it."

Carley smiled to herself as she turned to put the brisket into the kettle with two cabbages she had sliced. She then poured a small amount of water into the pan.

Sitting down at the table she put several washed white potatoes beside her, peeled them carefully, and cut them into small pieces to add to the beef and cabbage.

A kitten, Carley smiled, no one mean enough to push an old lady over a railing on the third floor would want a kitten. Neither Tillie nor Frances was the culprit, of that she was sure.

Twenty-five

T he doorbell rang, and Frances ushered in a tall, very lanky man doffing his hat and following her without hesitation through the hall to the dining room. He held a clipboard in one hand. After putting his hat on the top of the oven, he pulled a pencil from his shirt pocket and began making notes.

"Mr. Davenport," Carley greeted the house inspector she had seen several times over the years.

"Good morning, Miss Mertins," he said in a dour voice, probably the results of many years having to criticize landlords in less than perfect boarding conditions.

He slowly walked through each room on the first floor, making favorable comment on Carley's refurbished room. Upstairs, the first room he came to was Eulali's, and when he saw the pile of paperback books stacked on the floor against the wall, he turned to Carley.

"These books have to go. It seems that each time I come there is another pile of them. I guess she gets rid of them and then begins a new stack. They're a fire hazard. I know she doesn't smoke but a guest might. No, this isn't satisfactory at all. Tell her your license is in jeopardy if she doesn't stop hoarding all these books. Tell her to throw them out after she reads them. More than ten is unacceptable."

Mr. Davenport sat down and finished the notes. "Except for the books upstairs, everything is in order. Your license is fine for another year." After having Carley sign his report, he rose and walked back into the kitchen to retrieve his hat, turned on his heels, shook her hand, and marched through the hall and out the door. Carley felt like a whirlwind had just gone through the house. Frances and Tillie came up behind her.

"Well?" Frances asked.

"We're fine. Thanks to you two doing such a constant fine housekeeping job. However, we have to have Eulali get rid of 'those books'," all three of them said at once with a smile.

Breakfast was fairly quiet until Eulali joined the group. "Guess who I saw last night at the theater?"

"Who?" several chimed in at the same time.

"Horace Owens!" she smiled.

"Are you sure it was him? Did you talk to him?" Peter asked.

"Oh, yes. It was Horace. I didn't get to talk to him. I just saw him from the wings. When the show is going on I usually peep through the curtains at the audience. Last night wasn't a full house, it being a Thursday. Our biggest crowd is usually Saturday night. I guess all the folks think they can sin then and go to church the next morning and get right with the Lord."

"Good thinking," Larry said, "I hadn't thought of that."

"Well, he was sitting there in the third row between two ladies . . . I should say, Floozies from the looks of them."

"Are you sure?" Carley looked shocked.

"Oh, yes. Couldn't mistake that white hair of his. It was him. And he was having a great time. He didn't see me, I don't think."

"Oh, Eulali, I need to talk with you, if you have a minute after we're done eating. In the ballroom."

Eulali looked taken aback. "Oh, Miss Carley, I didn't mean to be gossiping," she protested.

"It's not that. Something entirely different."

Eulali looked relieved as she bent her head to the waffle in front of her, pouring on maple syrup.

After Frances and Tillie had taken all the dishes off the table, Carley and Eulali stepped into the ballroom through the small glass paned door that led directly from the dining room. Eulali stood silently until Carley had closed the door. Then, moving to the large Chesterfield sofa, they both sat down.

"The inspector was here yesterday, Eulali, and he said you have to get rid of that stack of books."

Eulali hung her head. "Yes, I know. He said the same thing last year, and I was going to sell them back to the used book place up on the Avenue. They cost me five cents for each 'used' book when I buy them, and then they buy them back when I finish them and return them. They pay me one cent each. Last year I had collected a hundred of them. I would have gotten a whole dollar for them!"

"Would have? What happened?" Carley asked curiously.

"Well, Mrs. Mertins took them all before I had a chance, and I found out she had taken them back and she kept the money . . . my money." Eulali's eyes darkened with anger. "She had no right."

"I'm sorry, dear," Carley tried to soothe her. "Why don't you do it this week? I don't think he'll come back to check, but I don't want to chance losing my license."

"How many do you think I can keep? There are a couple I'd like to always keep. They're Louis L'Amour westerns. Not all of them are the horror stories I like."

"I'd say you could keep a few." Carley put her hand to her head, deep in thought. "Up in the den there's a set of black marble book ends. Why don't you get them and put them on your bureau, and put your favorite between them? Surely, he can't object to a few books."

Eulali looked at Carley and tears sprang to her eyes. "Can I give you a hug?" she asked timidly.

"Of course, dear," Carley said reaching out her arms to the almost trembling lady.

After Eulali had gone, Carley sat thinking about the anger she had just witnessed from the little costume mistress. Yes, I guess she could get angry enough to do bodily harm. Perhaps.

⌒

Terry was waiting for Carley in the kitchen, a cup of steaming coffee in his hands.

"What can I do for you?" Carley smiled.

"First, a kiss and then I have something to ask. He put his arm around her shoulders as he set the cup on the table, and gave her a slow loving kiss which was interrupted by Frances coming into the room.

"Oops!" Frances said ready to turn on her heels and back out.

"Come on in, Frances," Terry invited, pulling away and sitting down next to his coffee cup.

"What did you want to talk to me about?" Carley asked, filling a cup for herself.

"When is Peter moving out of his room into Horace's?"

"Soon, but there's no date set. Why?"

"There's a young rookie in the force who wants to move out of his parent's house. Seems he has four sisters and now that he's earning his own money, he wants to get out from under all that femininity. Says he's tired of stockings hung over the towel racks in the bathroom."

"As long as you vouch for him, the room is his. I'll have to ask Peter when he is planning to make his move."

Carley had barely gotten the words out of her mouth when she heard Peter let out a whoop and "I knew it!" He came running into the room holding a small leather brief-case.

"What's that?" Terry asked.

"Found it in the window seat in Horace's old room. I don't think he ever knew the sill was a lid to a hollow box."

"What's in it?" Carley asked, reaching for the handle of the case.

"Have no idea. It's not mine, it's yours. None of my business." Peter let go of the case and sat down, obviously hoping Carley would open it and reveal its contents to him.

Instead, Carley placed the briefcase on the table and put her hand on it.

"Peter, I wonder when you thought you would be making your move into the new room. Terry has a new boarder in mind for your room."

"I can move out soon as I get back from my shift tonight, or first thing in the morning. It looks like you ladies did a thorough job getting my new room ready."

"Thank you, Peter. Thanks for finding the briefcase. I'll let you know if it holds a fortune. Maybe we can all quit work and live on easy street," she laughed.

Peter stood, ready to leave. "I told you this old mansion had secrets, didn't I?"

"You certainly did. Thanks!"

Peter left the room and Carley gingerly pushed a metal clasp aside on the leather case. It flopped open to reveal a sheaf of papers. She looked down at them and, one by one laid them out on the table. Several were clipped together making what looked like a ledger of business. They were written in the familiar hand of her great grandfather. It was an odd square-like signature she recognized from Christmas cards he had given her years and years ago. She had kept them in the scrapbook packed away in the attic. Aunt

Florence had never known she had that treasure. She would probably have thrown them away. She never said a good thing about her husband's father. Carley remembered him vaguely as a very loving and warm man.

One by one, the other papers revealed themselves to be I.O.U.s, not what he owed to others, but great sums owed to him. Carley sat back in her chair, looking past Terry to the wall, deep in thought, a redeeming realization slowly washing over her.

Tears brimmed in Carley's eyes, and she looked at Terry. "If all this means what I think it does, honey, you won't be marrying the great granddaughter of a womanizer and gambler."

"What do you mean?" Terry said, picking up one of the I.O.U.s."

Aunt Florence told me Great Grandfather lost the family fortune gambling and running around with loose women. I never had any real reason to not believe her, although somehow I never thought badly of him, but then I was very young when he died."

"Looking at this ledger and these unpaid notes, I'd say he was a very poor businessman and probably a soft touch." Terry mused. "It looks like these notes add up to a very large fortune."

"I imagine all these people who owed him money are long gone," Carley said, looking at the signatures and dates.

"I recognize one," Terry said. "He runs a shoe repair

shop down on F Street. Of course, it's not this guy but probably his great-grandson. Do you want me to check on it?"

Carley thought about it and shook her head. "You know, Terry. I think I'll honor my Great Granddaddy's wishes. He didn't push for payment and I'm pretty sure, even if we could trace these signatures and find the heirs, they probably don't have the money, nor do they know anything about them."

"I'm not even sure you could collect legally, even if you did find them," Terry spread his fingers through his hair in thought.

"Let's have a bonfire. Burn them, and be thankful Aunt Florence never found them. She would have relentlessly hounded each one to pay up."

"That's my girl. Besides, it's Christian to forgive. You are Christian, aren't you?" Terry smiled at her.

"I guess. I'm not a churchgoer, but, yes I suppose I do believe."

"Well, we'll be married in church, and I intend all our children are raised in the church. I belong to the Baptist persuasion."

"I thought all Irishmen were Catholic!" Carley looked surprised.

"Well, I guess most are. But when my ancestors found the Shenandoah Valley there weren't any Catholic churches around, so they went to worship in the nearest church, and it was a Baptist. We've been Baptist since."

Carley laughed. "That's fine with me. Just how many children are you thinking of?"

"I have an uncle and aunt, still up in the New York area, who have ten."

Carley's eyebrows lifted. "Forget it. I'm starting too late for that many."

Terry gave her a squeeze. "I agree. My salary wouldn't provide but for only a couple."

"Let's slow down a bit. We're not even married." Carley took a deep breath and looked down at the pile of papers. She set aside the ledger, scooped up the others and headed out the back door with the box of matches from the top of the oven.

Twenty-six

The September sky had just lightened when Terry and Wilbur started loading the trunk of the car parked near the gates to the alley behind Mertins Mansion.

"Put the easel in the back seat and the folded chair in the trunk," Terry suggested. "Then you'll have room in the trunk for everything else."

"Suits me," said Wilbur, reaching for a wooden box filled with paint tubes and brushes. A small palette was put into a cloth bag along with a small bottle of turpentine and another full of linseed oil.

"I think I have everything I'll need for a couple of days work on the farm down home. The only thing I'm taking is my shaving kit."

"Well, come in and eat breakfast before you go. No need traveling on empty stomachs." Carley stepped quickly across the dew dampened lawn and opened the back door. The aroma of fresh hot coffee wafted out the screen door, and Terry lifted his head and sniffed the air.

"Just when did you decide to go down to the valley?" Carley asked, reaching for three cups from the bottom shelf of the cabinet.

"Well," Terry explained, "Dan called me yesterday when I was at the apartment and asked me if I could come down for a couple of days. Seems he got all the hay mowing done and baled, but it needs two able-bodied men to get it all up into the barn lofts. Seems Dad wants to help and, of course, he's not really able yet. He won't admit it, so Dan needs me to help both convincing Dad and getting the hay put up."

"When did you talk to Wilbur?"

"Luckily, I bumped into him on the beat last night and asked if he'd like to go."

"Terry assured me Dan had already talked to Mrs. Clanahan, and she seemed willing to take on a guest," Wilbur smiled.

"He doesn't know it yet, but he'll be put to work slopping hogs and milking the cow," Terry laughed.

"You'll be surprised how adept I am at those chores," Wilbur grinned. "Years on Gramp's farm taught me well."

"Anyhow, honey," Terry smiled, taking the last gulp of coffee from his cup, "I'll be back Saturday night, and Wilbur will be down there until next Saturday. I'll make a quick rundown and come right back."

Wilbur looked at his wristwatch. "We'd better be going."

"Anxious to slop hogs?" Carley laughed as they walked out the back door.

"Be back in a couple," Terry said as he gave her a kiss on the cheek.

She gave them a wave as they pulled out the gate and disappeared out of sight. "I miss him already," she sighed.

⌒

The breakfast had just been served and Carley was buttering her toast when she turned to Peter who was sitting on her right.

"What is your schedule today?" she asked.

"I'm off until tomorrow noon. Why? Did you need me for something? I'm available," he quickly offered.

"Yes. I thought I'd take part of today to investigate the attic and perhaps clear out a lot of junk. Would you like to help?"

"You bet I would," he said eagerly.

"First off, then," Carley said, "Go up and open all the windows and get a cross air flow to clear out the heat. I'm certain it's too stuffy to work up there for a couple of hours."

Peter looked like he was going to get up right then when Carley grabbed his arm. "Eat your breakfast first. I have a couple of things to do before I can go up. Won't be long, though."

"Okay," Peter said as he settled back down in his chair and tackled his omelet with vigor.

⌒

When they got up the stairs from the third-floor landing and opened the door, they were greeted by a welcoming cool breeze from the open windows.

"Good," Carley sighed. "I was hoping for this. The last time I came here with Aunt Florence's things it was steaming hot. I broke out in a sweat before I had a chance to close the door."

"Where do we begin?" Peter asked, looking around the big sprawling room. Boxes and bags were everywhere.

"I should start with the bags first, but I am much too curious about what's in that big cedar chest over there. Let's start there."

"Suits me," Peter said on his way across the rough wood floor. "Do you want me to open it or do you want the honor?" he asked.

"You go ahead. I don't think it's locked."

Peter bent over and pulled the lid up without any trouble, while Carley discovered an old grey leather hassock nearby. It had a couple of slits in it.

"Don't know why this wasn't just thrown out instead of stored up here, but it will be a good perch for now.

Peering into the chest, Peter said, "Oh, Miss Carley, look at this pretty something!"

Carley looked and then picked up the lace work bundled there. "This is handmade, Peter. I don't know who, but somebody took a lot of time and loved to make it. Let's pull it out and see what it is."

They picked the lace up and it just kept getting larger and larger.

"Wow!" Peter was more and more amazed.

"It's a round tablecloth crocheted in the pineapple motif. Whoever did it put a lot of love and work into it."

"Is it supposed to be tan, or is it just old?"

"It's what they call ecru color. There are a few doilies in the ballroom in the same pattern, but they're white. Let's fold this up and put it aside on that end table by the door. I'll take it down with us to wash and try to restore it for use on the dining room table. I'll use it for very special occasions."

As they carefully folded it, Peter looked down and said, "Miss Carley! It's full of holes!"

Carley's heart missed a beat when she realized she had been the recipient of another of Peter's little jokes.

"Yes, Peter, I know, lots and lots of holes." Then, as she looked into the chest she caught her breath.

"What's the matter, Miss Carley?" Peter was concerned.

Carley kneeled beside the chest and brought out a Raggedy Ann doll. She sat back up on the hassock and hugged it to her, tears filling her eyes. Peter remained silent waiting for her to enlighten him.

With a big sigh, Carley looked up from the doll and shook her head.

"My mother gave me this doll for Christmas when I was eight, I think. I loved it and played with it, and even took her to bed with me. That Spring, I was playing in the yard and got it all muddy. Aunt Florence had told me to keep her clean. The next day I couldn't find my doll, and Aunt Florence told me she had thrown the filthy doll away." Carley paused for a moment before continuing, putting the doll up to her face. "I cried for days after that. Now, I find she hadn't thrown it away at all, but stuffed it up here in the attic."

"If I'd known this," Peter said quietly, "I'd probably have pushed her over that railing myself!"

Carley looked up at his face and could see the anger there.

"Oh well, it's over and done with," she looked back into the chest and saw a black lace parasol. She picked it up and started to open it.

"Don't do that," Peter warned. "Its bad luck to open an umbrella in the house."

"I'm not superstitious."

"Who would carry a black umbrella, anyway?"

"These were made for funerals. My guess is it was probably carried by one of my ancestors when one of my Great Grandpaps was buried." Just then, Carley let out a whoop and picked out a piece of cloth covered with colorful stitches.

"So that's what happened to it!" she exclaimed.

"What happened to what?" Peter came close to see.

"It's a sampler," Carley grinned.

"A what?"

"Well, when I was a little girl, it was what all little girls made to learn to sew. See, she pointed out some little knobby stitches in the center of a flower." "These are French knots," she explained "and these are backstitches, and these are satin stitches. All little girls were to make one, and then her folks would frame it and hang it on the wall so everyone could see and be proud. Mine was so bad, I thought they threw it away. Well, put it on the toss-out pile now," she laughed.

They kept digging through the chest and didn't discover anything more interesting than a few musty blankets, pillows and comforters.

"Some of these I can wash and give to the mission downtown. They're not very pretty, but they'll keep somebody warm this winter."

"You're a good person, Miss Carley," Peter smiled. "You always think of other people."

"I'm not that good, Peter. It's just that I hate to see anything go to waste. I guess you can say I'm cheap."

Peter laughed as he started going through a few of the boxes standing against one wall. One contained books. Lots of them.

"What will you do with these?" Peter asked picking up two of them.

"What are they?" Carley got up from the hassock and walked over to the box.

Looking down she noticed the top ones were novels, not schoolbooks. She stood there for a moment in deep thought.

Peter picked up a couple more books and laughed. "I bet Eulali would like to read a couple of these. There's two Sherlock Holmes mysteries right here on top."

"You're right, Peter. You know where they can go? Right behind the Morris chair in the ballroom. There's only a couple of figurines and a vase there now."

"I bet that's where these came from. It's ideal to have them within reach of sitting in that chair and reading."

"You're right, and that's just where you can put them."

Peter shoved the box over to the top of the steps and placed the crocheted tablecloth on top of it.

Carley looked at her watch. "It's getting close to lunch-time. I didn't realize how time has flown. We'll finish up in a couple of days. In the meantime, you can look into any-thing you want. I doubt you'll find any great treasures."

"Thank you, Miss Carley. I bet I'll find a Civil War me-mento. Just wait and see."

"I admire your optimism," Carley said as she lifted up the parasol and headed down the steps.

Yes, she said to herself, you're optimistic, Peter, but I haven't forgotten what you said about wanting to push Aunt Florence over the rail.

Twenty-seven

The house was in an early morning bustle. Peter was making trip after trip from his old to his new room with arms full of his clothes. He had to finish vacating his current digs before breakfast, or he would have to wait until he got back from his mid-morning shift.

He had already hauled boxes of books and hand tools. Carley had helped him carry a few smaller boxes of books and was not surprised when she read the titles, "Tips on Varnish", "Be a friend to your Handsaw", and "Be on the Level".

"Why am I not surprised by those book titles?" She asked him.

With a big grin and perspiration dripping from his nose, Peter was running up and down the stairs. "One day," Miss Carley. "One day. It's my dream."

"You'll be a really good cabinet maker, I know it."

"Thanks for your support," he said on his way back downstairs.

"I'll have to leave you," Carley called down to him. "Kitchen chores are waiting for me."

Eulali, too, was picking up bags and bags of books, leaving them in the hallway, ready to take them up the avenue to sell at the used book store.

"Breakfast is served," Frances informed both of them, and they stopped their labors and hurried down into the dining room, where the aroma of hot coffee filled the air.

"Eulali," Terry looked at the puffing lady as she sat down and swept away a rare stray lock of black dyed hair from her eyes. "How are you going to get those books up the Avenue?"

"I guess one bag at a time. I didn't make them very heavy."

"Well, if you wish, I'll take you up in my car, and it won't take long."

"Would you? It sure would help a lot. I'll get you a pass for the theatre," Eulali said gratefully, a big smile on her face.

"You forget, I can get in the theatre any time I want, Eulali. Thanks anyway," Terry chuckled.

"Just thought I'd offer," Eulali smiled stirring sugar into her coffee cup.

"Soon as we're done here, Eulali, let's you and me go up and find those book ends I told you about," Carley said. "They're in the den, but I'm not certain where. It's been a long time since I've spent much time up there."

Peter swallowed his last bite and turned to Carley. "I looked in that closet the other day, and I believe it has another slave room in the back of it." He pointed to the closet next to the black marble fireplace in the dining room.

"Really?" Carley's eyebrows went up as she spoke. "I always thought that closet wasn't very deep, but I never thought of that, even after you found the one in my room. Just didn't occur to me."

"If you let me, I think I can make space for a dumb waiter that would take things up to the landing on the second floor. Sure would help not to have to tote all those sheets, towels and stuff up and down the stairs, wouldn't it?"

"Let me think on that, Peter. Maybe we can look into it tomorrow or next week sometime."

"Okay. I have to get on to work right now, anyhow." He rose from the table, put his uniform visored hat on and left the room.

Carley turned to Eulali. "Soon as we get all the dishes cleared away, let's go up and get those book ends I told you about."

"All right. But when do you want to take the books up to the dealer, Terry?"

"You have time to get the bookends. I want to make a couple of phone calls first. May I use the phone in the hall, Carley?"

"Sure. We'll just be a few minutes."

When everyone had left the dining room on their way to their various jobs and things were settled down in the kitchen, Carley and Eulali climbed the stairs and faced the closed door to the upstairs den. When she pushed the door open, Eulali gasped.

"Miss Carley, this room is gorgeous. It's just beautiful!"

A Persian rug, intricate in design spread out before them.

Brilliant reds, dark and light blues and light tans, bordered and lightly fringed, covered over the floor leaving a border of polished oak flooring. A black marble mantle topped the fireplace. A mirror was framed in gold leafy glory, and it rose from mantle to ceiling. Two small shelves were on each side and cut china bowls sat on each.

A dark mahogany, glass-doored bookcase with two massive drawers at the bottom stood against the left wall, and a reading table holding a goose necked lamp sat beside it. On the opposite wall hung a large painting of a little girl walking beside a herd of cows with her hand on the neck of a little calf. She had a stick in her hand and wore a white pinafore. A cloudy sky over a dingy landscape backed up the cows and child.

"What a charming scene," Eulali remarked.

"Yes, I used to sit and look at that child for a long time when I was a little girl. How I longed to be her in that landscape, free and loved by a little animal. I was never allowed to have a pet like a dog or cat."

They stood looking at the picture for a few more moments before Carley shook her head and walked over to the chaise lounge. She picked up the bookends which were resting on a shelf above.

Eulali hugged them to her.

She reluctantly pulled her attention from the room and followed Carley out into the hall.

"I think I'll open the den for reading," Carley said, as they stepped to the floor of the hallway. "It would make a better study hall for Bucky than the ballroom with the radio or player piano interfering."

Terry had already loaded his car with the books, and he and Eulali swiftly stepped out the door and down to the street. Carley watched until the car pulled away from the curb before going back into the kitchen, where she intended making deep dish apple pie for dinner.

Carley had barely sat down at the kitchen table when the doorbell rang. She heard Tillie answer and then knock on Bill's door to announce to Larry that the cleaner's delivery man was there with Bill's suits and laundry, which Larry had taken for cleaning and washing two days before.

Carley smiled. Larry would spend the next couple of minutes putting safety pins in collars and belt loops for Bill.

Just as she thought things were quieting down, Carley heard a rumble of thunder in the distance.

I hope Terry and Eulali get back before it rains, Carley thought to herself. She anxiously watched the clock and was relieved when she heard the front door open and heard their voices. Eulali went upstairs to get ready for work and Terry came into the kitchen, two bottles of grape Nehi in his hands.

"Thought you'd like a little bit of refreshment," he said handing one cold bottle to her.

"That was very thoughtful. Thanks," Carley smiled. Her spirits, which for some reason had been at a low ebb all morning, were somewhat lifted.

"What's the matter, honey?" Terry asked concerned.

"I don't know really," Carley answered taking a sip of soda from the bottle. "I guess it's not being able to solve Aunt Florence's murder."

"Oh, that," Terry looked down at his drink and shook his head. "I've spent many minutes on the beat thinking about it, and I haven't been able to come up with an answer, either."

"I think I let the real culprit go when I made Horace Owens leave the house."

"I think so, too, dear. Then, again, how on earth could we prove he did it? You would need a witness to testify to it, wouldn't you?"

"I guess so. I've pretty much eliminated everyone else. I know there was a lot of animosity between Aunt Florence and almost all the boarders, at one time or another, and it still bothers me, but I know I can't keep fretting over it forever."

"That's my girl," Terry said as a timid knock was heard at the door to the kitchen.

Looking up they saw Wilbur standing there with some canvases in his arms.

"Can I come in?" he asked timidly.

"Of course. What do you have there?" Terry asked.

"These are three of the pictures I painted while down at your parent's house last week." He held them out one by one and laid them on the table. One was a fairly large landscape full of reds, oranges, and yellows and sunshine.

"It is beautiful," Carley gasped. "You really outdid yourself on this one."

A smaller one depicted the stream running through the lower acreage behind the blacksmith shop. The third one made Terry draw in his breath as he looked at a lady, he couldn't see her face under the poke bonnet she wore, feeding chickens out in the yard.

"That's Ma," he almost whispered. "You did a wonderful job, Wilbur. A wonderful job. How much do you want for them?"

"Nothing," Wilbur smiled. "These are yours on your wedding day. Not before."

"Guess I'll have to marry the lady," Terry joked. "This just gives me three more reasons."

Carley felt her spirits lift just as the sky darkened and a loud clap of thunder split the heavens, and rain poured down in what seemed to be buckets. Wilbur scooped up the pictures in his arms.

"The next time you see these, they'll be in frames." With that he disappeared through the dining room, and they heard him on the stairs.

Carley looked at Terry, concern in her eyes. "Do you think he heard what we were talking about when he was at the door?"

"Don't know. I have no idea how long he had been standing there."

"I certainly hope he didn't hear."

Twenty-eight

The rain, which had started the day before had continued overnight, seemingly put a shroud of gloom over the house. Usually on Saturday, everyone had plans for going out, visiting or doing some window shopping. Even Carley's opening of the beautiful den upstairs hadn't really lifted spirits, for sheets of water continually washed down the large window panes.

She had announced the availability of the room at lunch. Eulali had gone overboard describing it.

"It really sounds nice and quiet for home work," Bucky said and then asked, "What kind of books are in the bookcase?"

"Not sure, Bucky, but I do know there are a couple wonderful ones on the stars and planets. They're illustrated. My grandfather used to take me out in the backyard at night to look at the Big Dipper and Venus."

"How old were you?" Terry asked.

Only about five, I think. He died when I was pretty little."

Breakfast, usually very chatty and spirited, had been like a sigh, as everyone consumed their food deep in their own thoughts, not sharing them with others. Everyone in the house was there to say goodbye to Larry, who was packed and ready to leave after lunch. The rain had stopped, but still, the sun refused to shine.

Even Frances and Tillie seemed to have their minds on other things. They had spent the morning cleaning Peter's old room, and even then, their only remarks were how neat the man was. They had hardly needed to dust. Somehow, Carley wasn't surprised, knowing how clean he had been painting her room.

Terry was to bring the rookie to dinner, and Carley hoped he wouldn't get the wrong idea of what his fellow boarders would be like, although, she was sure Terry already told him all about them.

"Let's just put out the makings of sandwiches, girls," Carley suggested, instead of making them up. There's egg salad and chicken salad in a bowl in the fridge. Slice some of those nice tomatoes from the valley and pull apart and wash a head of lettuce. Everyone can make their own."

"Do you want us to cut that pie for lunch?" Tillie asked, her eyes looking hungrily at the two brown-crusted peach pies standing on the butcher-block table.

"Yes, of course," Carley answered. "And that should be enough."

She looked around as Terry and the rookie appeared on the stoop outside the screen door. They took off their wet yellow slickers and hung them on hooks under the roof overhang to drip dry.

"This is Woodrow Kurtz," Terry spoke to Carley by way of introduction.

"Glad to meet you, Mr. Kurtz," Carley smiled and turned to the ladies busy with lunch.

"These ladies are Frances Jones and Tillie Lincoln, Woody." Terry introduced them.

Both ladies looked up and smiled and the young man nodded. Blonde curly hair seemed to bob up and down over a face decorated with a small neat mustache. His pale blue eyes seemed to sparkle with humor.

"Please call me Woody," he turned to Carley. "I hope you'll take me on as a boarder. I've heard nothing but praise about this place, including the cooking. Officer Clanahan is quite fond, I believe, of both you and the food."

Carley blushed and laughed. "He's full of Irish blarney, so don't believe everything he says. And please call me Carley. We're very informal here."

Turning to Terry she said, "Really, Terry, you didn't have to bring him here through the alley and backyard," she chided him.

"That means every place else gets better!" Terry pinched her cheek lightly.

"Let's go into the dining room, Woody," Terry led the young man in and introduced him to everyone.

"Bill is our Braille typist, Larry is his safety pin brother, Peter is our carpenter bus driver, Bucky is our studious one, and Eulali is our gem of a burlesque queen."

"Hello everyone," Woody smiled, almost embarrassed

by Terry's flippancy. "I'm Woody, the bumbling rookie. I'll let you know before Terry tells," he laughed.

As everyone was finishing lunch in the dining room, Carley looked up as Peter left the room. He then returned with a large crowbar in his hand.

"Found this in the cellar," he said opening the closet door and pulling out the carpet sweeper with the "Hoover" logo on the big grey bag hanging in front.

Carley put out her hand to stop him, hoping to put off the destruction of the closet until after lunch, when with one great effort the ancient door came off its hinges at the back of the closet and fell to the floor.

What happened next seemed to occur in slow motion. A skeleton dressed in Navy Blues fell out onto the dining room floor. The skull, topped with a white hat askew over one eye, bounced and stopped rolling, only to look up at Carley from its position at her feet.

The room was silent for a very brief moment when Tillie screamed and fainted, sending a tray of lunch plates and forks crashing to the floor, scattering everywhere.

Eulali stood quickly and gurgled a queer sound as she put both palms to her mouth and headed to the bathroom. The whole room then emitted a group gasp at the ghoulish scene, with Bill asking, "What happened?" When no one answered immediately, he repeated over and over, "What happened?" until Larry sat down beside him to explain a skeleton had fallen out of the closet.

"A what?" Bill yelled in disbelief.

Buddy growled, but didn't bark, and he nestled closer to his master. The whole room exploded with questions and remarks.

Terry put his arms around Carley and made her sit down, and then took charge of the ghastly situation.

With arms held high, he quieted the room with his authority.

"Folks, please . . . all of you . . . go into the ballroom and wait. Frances will serve you sandwiches shortly. Take your drinks with you. Soon as I can, I'll be in to report on things."

Woody bent over Tillie and helped Frances get her to her feet. One on each side of her, they took her to the kitchen to get her a glass of water and sit her down in the rocking chair.

"I'll clean up the broken dishes," Woody volunteered. "Where's the broom and dustpan?"

Frances smiled and showed him, as she returned her attention to Tillie, who was still shaking as she recovered her wits.

Back in the dining room, Terry was squatting beside Carley as she sat staring back at the macabre skull grinning up at her feet.

"He's smiling at me," she whispered to Terry.

"Looks a bit like that. Oh, look, there's a note pinned to his middy." Terry got up, reached over and unpinned the note and handed it to Carley.

"It's your skeleton, honey. You read it." He tried to lighten the scene that looked so somber.

Carley gingerly opened the old yellowed paper and spread it out on her lap.

"It's in Aunt Florence's handwriting!" She gasped.

"Are you sure?"

"Yep. Listen, I'll read it to you." Carley took a deep breath and began. "To whom it might concern. This man is Darnell Eubanks. He is the father of Evelyn's bastard. He came here two days after she was born and wanted to see her. I asked him if he was going to marry my daughter, and he told me he couldn't, for he already had a wife. I asked him if he wanted a cup of tea before going upstairs, and when he said he did, I sat him down and served him a cup of tea strongly laced with arsenic. He died quickly, and I put his body in the closet and caulked the door shut tight. I write this note so that no one else could get credit for killing this no-good lowlife.

"It's signed Florence Mertins," Carley said in barely a whisper, and then it dawned on her.

"Oh, my, Terry. I'm looking at my father!"

"And he's looking up at you, too," Terry almost laughed.

"It's not really a laughing matter," Carley said. "Do you realize that somewhere there's a widow of over a quarter of a century who never knew what happened to her husband?"

"You're right, honey." Terry was aware Carley had immediately become concerned for someone else's widow.

He felt so proud of her. "It probably won't be too hard to find her, since we know who he is, and the Navy will have records of him. They probably looked for him as a deserter for a while."

Carley stood, and as she turned, she saw Wilbur standing in the doorway. His shoulders were bent in what looked like total dejection. His eyes fixed on the skeleton.

"Miss Carley, may I talk to you and Officer Terry?"

"Of course. What's wrong? That is besides a skeleton on the floor? Carley almost laughed at the incongruity of the situation.

"I overheard what you were saying yesterday, and it's time for me to confess."

"Confess what?" Terry asked softly as though he knew what was coming.

"I killed Mrs. Mertins. I pushed her over the railing. I didn't really mean to, but I did."

"You?" Carley asked, astonished.

"She came upstairs that morning to change the light bulb. I came out of my room with that canvas of the vase from the den. She saw it and became very angry at me. Told me I was a thief, and she was going to call the police.

"I reminded her that the vase had been put back, and then she said that if I gave her half the money I got from any picture I sold with any of her property in it, she'd forget my thievery. When I refused, she took the light bulb and pushed it in my face, using such bad language. I just pushed her to get her out of my face." Wilbur took a deep breath.

"I guess I pushed her too hard. She went backward, broke the rail and fell. I didn't mean to, but I did kill her."

He looked so dejected Carley was sure he was going to cry. She got up and put her arms around his shoulders.

"I just couldn't let you go on fretting over this," Wilbur added, "And I didn't want you thinking that nice Horace Owens did it. I guess you want to arrest me, Terry."

Terry looked at Carley and she nodded to him with a smile. Terry knew exactly what she was thinking.

"Wilbur, this case was deemed an accident a few months ago. It was just that. I doubt anyone downtown would be happy about re-opening the case. It was accidental, and accidental it will remain."

Wilbur wiped tears from his face with a large white handkerchief he pulled from his back pants pocket. He blew his nose loudly and sat down obviously exhausted by the afternoon's events.

Carley looked up at Woody standing by the door as Frances walked through with a large tray of sandwiches with a broad smile on her face.

"Welcome to Mertins Manor, Woody," Carley laughed. Woody put his hand up to his forehead in a bright snappy salute.

Epilogue

Eulali West retired from the Costume Mother position at the Gayety and moved to her sister's farm in Maryland. The peace and quiet got to her, and within six months, she moved to New York City and got an apartment near the hustle and bustle of Broadway. She met a "stage door Johnny", married him and they spent the rest of their lives watching shows from seats in the audience, instead of peeking through the curtains in the wings.

⌣

Bill Wampler moved in with his brother when Buddy died of old age. He later got another seeing-eye-dog that he named Buddy III. It seems the Buddy he had at the Manor was his second dog. Carley heard from Larry on occasion, and he assured her Bill was doing fine.

⌣

Peter Roberts never did marry his Roberta. Instead, he met the young lady who worked as a bookkeeper in a department store when she road frequently on his bus. They married and moved into her apartment on 16th Street. Before he left Mertins manor he installed the dumb waiter in the dining room closet. He then retired from the bus company and became a cabinetmaker.

⌣

Bucky Keller went to Johns Hopkins and became a doctor, married one of the high kicker chorus girls he had met at the burlesque, and became a family doctor back home in Morgantown. Carley never did get a report on what his mother thought about the daughter-in-law, but Bucky did say she was happily reconciled about his becoming a doctor instead of a pharmacist. He frequently got behind the lunch counter and proved his skills as a soda jerk with his younger patients.

⌣

Horace Owens was often seen with a lady on his arm parading around town. It was evident his insurance business was still intact, or else the ladies were wealthy. One can only speculate.

⌣

Woody Kurtz became the first of many police officers to find room and board at the Manor. In fact, Carley never did have to put a "vacancy" sign in the window again.

⌣

Jolie and Frances served Carley into their old age. Tillie left when her first baby was born, and she and Stan went to live with his folks. From reports, it was a very happy arrangement. Stan became a well-known attorney and supported his folks in their old age.

⌣

Wilbur became a permanent part of Terry's family in the valley, where he helped with the farm work and painted beautiful landscapes that became very popular throughout the country, as well as D.C. He would often stay for a few days in the "Maid's room" over the kitchen in the Mansion. He'd go out to offices and street corners, and was quite successful at a period when times were hard.

⌣

Carley had her musicals in the ballroom, but they weren't classical. She always said Aunt Florence would turn over in her grave if she could hear the harmonica, fiddle, guitar and sax music that resounded from the walls and out into the hallway.

Terry and Carley married and had three children, twin boys and a girl. Carley kept the rooms downstairs for family, and only rented out the upstairs to her "uniformed family" as she called them.

During World War II, Terry enlisted in the Navy and spent four years on a destroyer. He returned home happily unscathed with his old job waiting for him. As in the story books, he, Carley and family lived happily ever after.

Carley's father—or his skeleton—was returned to his brother's family for a Christian burial. His wife's family did not want anything to do with the "sailor philanderer." After seven years, his wife had remarried and was living happily without him.

About the Author

Phyllis Wood Fravel was born in Pennsylvania on December 7, 1926, but she spent her childhood in the row houses of northwestern Washington, D.C. A talented musician, her mother dreamed of her becoming a concert pianist, but World War II redirected her path. Working for the wartime federal government, she met her future husband while taking night classes. The two moved briefly to the Shenandoah Valley before settling in Woodbridge, Virginia, to raise five children.

Fravel is a lifelong artist with many interests. An accomplished pianist, she has played for a variety of northern Virginia churches from the age of twelve, while also indulging a love of watercolor and oil painting. Writing, however, has been a passion she has enjoyed her entire life. She has published numerous times, including a regular political column for the "Potomac News" in the 1960s and 1970s. With a number of manuscripts completed, this is her first published novel.

CPSIA information can be obtained
at www.ICGtesting.com
Printed in the USA
BVOW06*1728160118
504702BV00005B/2/P